PURITAN ADVENTURE

PURITAN ADVENTURE

Written and Illustrated by

LOIS LENSKI

J.B. Lippincott Company

Philadelphia & New York

"And truly there is no pleasure comparable to a generous spirit."

CAPTAIN JOHN SMITH,
*Advertisements for the Un-
experienced or The Path-way
to Erect a Plantation.* 1631

Foreword

My research has included available original sources and first-hand accounts by early explorers, by the two Governors, Bradford and Winthrop, and others. No study of early Puritan life, however, is complete unless it includes research regarding the background in England—the counties of Essex and Sussex—from which the first Massachusetts settlers came.

The contrast between the Old English and the New English backgrounds is startling, and one aspect of it has been overlooked in our reconstructions of Puritan life. We must remember that the men and women of the first generation had lived as boys and girls in this freer, "merrier" Old England. Alice Morse Earle, in her book Margaret Winthrop, *speaks of "that first generation whose numbers had not all been born to an inheritance of Puritan soberness, whose fathers had lived in the joyous and glowing sunlight of the Elizabethan epoch, and who had known how to be merry in their day." The restrictions and repressions of Puritan life were largely assumed therefore, after they had reached manhood and womanhood. Due to variations in human nature, they were not all equally willing, the moment they set foot on these shores, to don the mantle of austerity and harshness. Hence, my belief that such a character as Aunt Charity may have been possible.*

One early explorer mentions that the English fishermen who visited the New England coast often "planted a Maypole on the sandy beach and danced round it." So we may assume that Morton's famous Maypole at Merrymount was not the only one set up on these shores.

It is a well-known fact that the celebrations of May Day and Christmas in Old England were times of disorderliness and drunkenness. The Puritans in New England deliberately instituted Thanksgiving Day and Election Day to take their place. The celebration of Christmas was not revived until the middle or, in some parts of New England, the latter half of the nineteenth century.

The early writers tell us practically nothing of child life, but we know that in the training and care of children seventeenth-century English customs were followed. The beating of children by parents and schoolmasters was so com-

mon a practice, even to a much later date, that it was not considered as cruel or shocking as it seems to us today.

In the punishment of crime, New England was less harsh than other parts of the world at this period. Whereas Old England had some thirty crimes punishable by death, New England had only ten. There are no known recorded cases of duckings in New England, although it is believed that certain towns possessed ducking stools. Their use would have aroused no surprise, because the ducking stool was a common instrument in Old England at this time.

I have been obliged to simplify legal procedure in the Massachusetts Bay Colony to make it more understandable to young readers. "The town Court" which I describe would probably have been a hearing, at which the magistrate, as justice of the peace, could hear petty cases. The more serious cases, those involving arson, or those punishable by whipping or ducking, would have been tried by jury in the quarterly court held at the county seat.

"Know-God" was a real Indian boy, who after the death of many Indians of the Massachusetts tribe, including Sachem Chickatawbut, by small-pox, was kept by the English. He was adopted by Governor Winthrop himself, and is mentioned in the latter's Journal.

I have incorporated in my story many quotations taken from the early New England writers. It is these phrases, so rich and suggestive, in the original sources, which give this long-past age a glow of reality and truth. In them we hear our founders speak, think and act. They are the rightful heritage of American children, and have a rightful place in a book of their own.

FOREWORD

Every effort has been made to present an authentic picture, both in text and illustrations, of the Puritans and the tribe of Massachusetts Indians. I have chosen to describe an imaginary town instead of a real one, in order to present a composite and therefore more typical picture of life in the Massachusetts Bay Colony about the year 1635. The Pioneers' Village erected in Salem, Massachusetts, in 1930, an authentic reproduction of a Puritan village of 1630, showing the types of shelter built by the first settlers and in use at the time of the arrival of Governor Winthrop, has served in a general way as the model for my village. Descriptive material regarding the same has been freely used. To any one interested in early Puritan life, a visit to the Pioneers' Village is invaluable.

Chapter V, DAY OF WORK AND NO CHEER, was first written as a short story for THE SHINING TREE AND OTHER CHRISTMAS STORIES, published by Alfred A. Knopf, Inc., and is reprinted here with their permission.

Lois Lenski

Greenacres
  Harwinton, Connecticut

CONTENTS

CHAPTER ONE

Good News

"A sail! A sail!" The cry came from a dark-skinned, half-grown boy, who flew fleet as the wind, past the open door. His long arm, upraised, pointed toward the open sea.

Goodwife Partridge and her children hastened out.

"Today it comes!" announced Seaborn, the eldest boy, solemnly.

"Who was it? What said he?" cried the Goodwife.

"'Twas Know-God, the Indian boy," explained Seaborn. "The long-awaited ship from England cometh at last."

1

"Know-God hath seen a sail!" piped up little Waitstill.

Goodwife Partridge held God-be-thanked, the babe, on one arm. She lifted her hand to shade her eyes.

The late October sun shone softly upon the group before the low, straw-thatched cottage. It bathed in mellow warmth the fort on the hill as well as the houses that lined the winding path and clustered at the water's edge. It traced in shining light the course of the river making its way to the blue sea beyond.

"I see naught!" cried Goodwife Partridge, in vexation. "A few fishing shallops near shore and naught else."

"But Know-God's eyes be black as jet!" cried Waitstill, in excitement. "Black eyes be strongest for sight. Pale blue eyes like ours cannot see half so well."

"But the Crier—hath he cried the ship?" asked Goodwife Partridge. "See you the Crier, childer? Hear you his bell?"

"Oh, Ma'am, will Aunt Charity come?" asked eight-year-old Comfort.

"Will the ship bring her?" echoed Thankful, her sister, but one year younger.

The two girls might have been twins, except that one was shorter than the other. Like their mother, they were dressed in Puritan costume, long full petticoats and tight-fitting waistcoats of russet-colored cloth, relieved by calico aprons and falling collars. White lawn coifs or caps fitted close to their shapely heads.

"Know-God's eyes be, indeed, far-seeing," said Seaborn sternly. "Parson Humphrey saith he hath the intelligence of the Devil. He hath oft told of a ship at sea, which he hath seen sooner by one hour, yea two hours, than any

English man that stood by of purpose to look out."

The little group stood silent, their eyes strained toward the brightness of the sea. Behind them a crude fence of split palings enclosed a tiny yard where, on both sides of the trim clam-shell path, grew a few straggling vegetables and herbs.

A stir of activity began along shore. Men and boys appeared on the wharves which had been empty before. Running figures moved swiftly along the descending paths. People looked out of doors and windows. The seaport came to life.

"Look ye! The sail! I see it plain!" cried Waitstill.

A white speck could now be seen against the blue. Soon it was in the bay, growing larger and whiter each moment. Then the clang of a bell rang out.

"Good news! Good news!" came the Town Crier's shout. "A ship from England . . . a ship from England docks this day!"

Up the grassy path strode the stooped and bent figure of a man, bell in hand. His voice was harsh, his bell-clang harsher, and his face belied the welcome of his news. Sour and cross he looked, as if he grudged the bringing of cheer and hated all happiness.

"Go ye, find your father, lads," said Goodwife Partridge quickly. "He works with the thatchers in the marsh grasses along the beach. Tell him the news—a ship cometh. He will do well to fetch home fresh fish or game for supper."

The two boys hurried off.

"Will then our Aunt Charity come?" asked Comfort again.

But Goodwife Partridge's heart was too full for answer. Food and clothing, letters and news of dear ones—a ship from home meant all these things. But this time more, perhaps. Perhaps sister Charity *would* be aboard. Little Charity, left behind a mere child in England, ten years before. Now a woman grown, a woman young in years, but old enough to have borne the sorrow of loss of both their parents and of her newly married husband.

It was now a year since Goodwife Partridge had had Parson Humphrey write the letter which bade her come out to her sister in the new world. There had been no reply. Each ship brought the hope that Charity might come, but she had not. A new ship meant new hope. Would Charity come and would her sister know her if she came?

Goodwife Partridge made haste to the kitchen to stir up an extra batch of Indian bannock and set it on a board before the open fire. With the birch-twig broom, Thankful hastily swept stray ashes from the great stone hearth. Comfort ran, at her mother's bidding, and brought a piggin of water brimful from the spring hard by the kitchen door.

Goodwife Partridge grasped the ladle and stirred briskly the pumpkin sauce which simmered and bubbled in the great iron pot.

"I fear 'twill burn, with no one to mind it," she said.

"I will bide at home, Ma'am," said Thankful, "and stir the pumpkin sauce."

"Ay, 'tis well, daughter. Bide ye here. Comfort goes with me to mind the babe."

The wharf was packed when the good ship *Fearless* dropped anchor alongside. A brave sight she was, with her great cabin, lofty poop, fighting tops, lateen-rigged mizzen, whipstaff and high forecastle. But the thin-faced passengers looked worn and weary as, with outstretched arms and glad cries, they leaned far out over the rail. The waves slapped against the gunwale, the sailors tugged at the ropes, and while seagulls cried mournfully overhead, the passengers stepped ashore.

"Charity hath bonny blue eyes and brown hair that curls. Her cheeks were ever ruddy—I see her yet. Always merry, always skipping and running she was. We called each other 'Madcap' and 'Mischief' for pet names. Sometimes graver people called her a *hoyting* girl, but she meant no one harm . . ."

Her mother spoke as if to herself, but Comfort listened happily. Of this unknown aunt she never tired hearing.

The townspeople fell back as the newcomers appeared. A woman with three children was noisily welcomed by the Hatherly family. A group of tradesmen, loaded down with tools, were met by the town authorities. An old man, a young couple with a boy at their side, a gentleman and his lady before whom the others stepped aside—these were the newcomers. A babble of greetings, tears and sobs of recognition and welcome, laughter of relief and fear filled the air.

Loud words were bandied back and forth:

"How good to leave the evil-smelling ship and taste the air!"

"A cup of New England's air be better than a whole draught of Old England's ale!"

"The air be sweet! The smell of land be sweet!"

"If this land be not rich, then is the whole world poor."

"Have ye no houses built for us? Where then can we live?"

"No place for those of a dronish disposition . . ."

"So many godly persons were going . . ."

"Our hands be coarse. Here there is work to do."

"God hath brought us safe to land . . ."

"From a paradise of plenty into a wilderness of wants."

"What sound greets my ear? The cry of wild animals in the forest? Ye have lions here that roar?"

"It is a country rather to affright, than to delight one."

"God hath preserved us through our afflictions . . ."

"Have ye no town? No town houses? Only crude hovels at the door of the forest? Ye call this a thriving settlement?"

Comfort Partridge held tight to her small brother's hand, as the words smote her ears.

The seamen hastened out, bringing their goods on shore.

"She hath not come," said Goodwife Partridge sadly. "Wait ye here. I needs must buy lace and hooks and eyes if the seamen's price be not too dear."

She went to the corner of the warehouse where hasty counters of planks had been set up and villagers and seamen began noisily bickering.

Comfort waited with a sinking heart. She wanted Aunt Charity to come. Somehow she knew that Aunt Charity would be different from anyone she had known before. Although she had never seen her, she knew she would greatly love her. But Aunt Charity had not come. A tear stole down her cheek.

"The wind blew mightily, the sea roared, the waves

tossed us horribly, but God in his mercy saved us. Scores of cattle were so tossed and bruised they straightway died." It was the Captain of the *Fearless* speaking.

"How many brought ye?" asked the Magistrate.

"With a brave hundred we started out," growled Captain Boswell. "But three months' battling with storms killed scores, I say."

"What provision brought ye?" The Magistrate s voice was stern.

"When the storms raged, we had to empty great supply of provision and extra store overboard, I tell ye!"

"Overboard!" echoed the Magistrate. "How then shall we feed these people?"

Townsmen crowded close and a general hubbub arose. Comfort watched the scrawny cattle being dragged off the ship by scolding cowkeepers.

"What mechanics brought ye?" demanded the Magistrate. "We be in sore need of an ingenious carpenter and a cunning joiner. Have ye brought out a good brickmaker, a leather dresser, a handy cooper and a weaver to weave fine cloth? These we have sent for repeatedly."

"Some died on the voyage—'twas the brickmaker, methinks," replied Captain Boswell, scratching his head. "Or, was it the weaver? There they be yonder," he pointed. "Go ask 'em which died."

The Magistrate turned to the mechanics, but the Captain called him back. "Have ye then good store of salt fish ready? Clapboard and beaver hides for my voyage back to Old England?" But he got no answer.

Little God-be-thanked began to whimper. Comfort took him in her arms. Once more Aunt Charity had not come. The disappointment was hard to bear.

A sudden commotion arose.

"Ye sneak! Ye naughty baggage! I catched ye!"

A seaman appeared, dragging a half-grown, unkempt girl by the arm. Fighting like a tiger, the girl turned and bit the man's arm. He dropped her wrist like a hot coal. Then he cornered her between a pile of barrels and the building.

"Ye won't get away scot-free, no ye won't! Hey, Cap'n Boswell, look ye here at this wench. She's a tryin' to skip without so much as a by-your-leave!"

The Captain and the Magistrate hurried over. The Constable appeared and several tithing-men. Comfort came closer, holding the babe tightly in her arms.

The girl wore no coif or neck-cloth. Her hair fell over her eyes, as her head hung forward with a hang-dog air. She carried a kerchief-tied bundle of clothing. Her petticoat and apron were soiled and torn. She must be a very wicked person, to appear so distraught.

"Hold her fast!" snorted Captain Boswell, in a low voice. "She hath made life miserable for every passenger on board —she hath stolen bisket-cake by the barrel, she hath thieved seven precious lemons and eat them all at one sitting. She hath proved herself a devil of a nuisance." Aloud he shouted: "Here's a husky, fourteen-year-old female, a bargain for anyone who needs a strong-armed servant gal! Who will pay passage for this likely redemptioner?"

The crowd closed in and Comfort was pushed aside. "She hath a sinful heart. How wicked she must be. Who would want a wicked servant?" said Comfort to herself.

Then she saw a fair lady talking to the Captain. Above the crowd she saw the lady's black beaver hat. Below, she caught a glimpse of her gown of fresh flaming silk. Would so fine a lady pay passage for so wicked a servant?

She saw Gaffer and Goodwife Lumpkin hasten up and melt into the crowd. Goody Lumpkin had an unsavory reputation. Her tongue was as sharp as a scissors blade and she never gave it rest. Poor Gaffer Lumpkin led a sorry life and a silent one. They had no children, so Goody Lumpkin longed for a servant. Well, if she bought this one, she might have her hands pretty full. Comfort turned to go.

Then she heard the lady speaking.

"She is but a child. If treated fairly, the best side of her nature can be brought out."

The lady's words were clear and sweet. Her face, turned toward Comfort for a moment, made the child's heart skip a beat. The glance reminded her of something warm and sweet and familiar, she knew not what.

"Evil we punish here in New England," answered the Magistrate.

"She hath had enough of brutality in her short life,"

retorted the lady. "Why not try kindness? It might save her soul!"

The Magistrate looked the lady up and down. He frowned at her costly apparel. The very color of her shining gown seemed to hurt his eyes.

"Kindness!" he exclaimed. "Punish wrong-doing with kindness!" He jerked the cringing girl to her feet. "Captain Boswell," he shouted, "why brought ye here this wench? We have no place for corrupt and naughty persons in our fair town. Back to England she must go!"

"Never!" replied the Captain. "Some godly woman can

make of her a useful servant maid."

"Mistress, wilt buy her yourself?" The Magistrate turned to the lady.

Before she could reply, the two Lumpkins rushed forward.

"No, no, buy her not!" screamed Goody Lumpkin, in haste. Then in a politer tone she added: "Oh, good sir, 'tis *we* who want her." With her sharp elbow she poked her husband in the ribs. "Say what I telled ye to say."

"We take her home . . . my wife, she needeth a goodly serving maid," piped up Gaffer Lumpkin obediently. "I pay her passage money, if she serve us for five years and I give her a she-goat to help her start out in life."

"No, no, no, no!" screamed the girl. She broke away and with outstretched arms, fell imploring at the lady's feet. "Don't let them take me, Ma'am! Don't!"

The lady leaned over and spoke to the girl, whereupon she rose quietly to her feet. Captain Boswell and the Lumpkins talked together and soon the Lumpkins went away with the redemptioner held tightly between them. She tossed her hair aside and looked back once at the lady in the silken gown. Now hath Goody Lumpkin a servant to her liking, thought Comfort.

The Magistrate again looked the lady up and down.

"No place here for those of a dronish disposition, who come in the hope to live in plenty and idleness. No place here for those that would live off the sweat of another man's brows." The words were as harsh and biting as a wintry wind out of the north. "All must be workers in some kind."

The lovely lady bowed her head a trifle. "So I have heard."

"Why then come ye here?" The Magistrate's question was blunt.

"I am a widow, good sir." The lady lifted her chin. "My husband dying so soon after the death of my father and mother . . . my sister sent for me to come out . . ." Her voice trembled and her eyes looked uncertainly about.

"It is the duty of widows and spinsters to serve the whole settlement; to show mercy with cheerfulness and to minister to the sick and poor brethren. See ye to it." The Magistrate started to go but turned back. "Your name then, Mistress?"

"Widow Cummings, sir," replied the lady. "My sister . . ."

Comfort saw her mother coming. Goodwife Partridge, unable to buy the needed articles, hurried back.

"God-be-thanked hath been well-behaved, Ma'am," reported Comfort. "He hath not cried once."

But her mother looked not at her babe, nor did she listen. She saw only the lady standing so still beside the Magistrate. The two women looked at each other, then fell into each other's arms.

"Sister!" cried the fair lady.

"Charity! Dear Charity!" sobbed Goodwife Partridge.

"Aunt Charity hath come at last," said Comfort softly.

CHAPTER TWO

A Strange
Land This

Comfort came to the attic chamber early the next
morning. "The neighbors be come to see you,
Aunt!" she said.

"What wild roars and loud wailing heard I through the
night?" asked Aunt Charity. "Some said on the *Fearless* ye
have lions here that roar. Is it true, Comfort?"

"Father says some have seen a lion at Cape Ann," replied

Comfort. "He hath seen skins of all other beasts save only lions."

"It howled so fierce, it did affright me," Aunt Charity went on. " 'Twas not a lion then?"

"No, Aunt, 'twas not a lion."

With sober face, Comfort glanced at the bed, where lay bright-colored garments with trimmings of lace and embroidery. Aunt Charity picked up several things and together they went down the narrow stairs. Comfort sat silently down on a block in the corner. She took up a red stocking she was knitting.

"My sister, Widow Cummings, gossips," announced Goodwife Partridge proudly.

"It gladdens our hearts to see you!" cried Mistress Seward. She stepped forward and grasped Aunt Charity's hands in her own. Then came the others, Mistress Hollingworth, Mistress Cartwright, Goodwives Pitkin, Minching, Rogers, Perkins and Lumpkin.

"Tell us news of Old England!" begged the women.

"The grass is green, the flowers bloom bravely, the lark still soars and sings in the heavens," said Aunt Charity softly. She sat down in a chair and continued: "It seems only yesterday I was there in my father's old home in Essex. The roses were a-bloom in the bed beside the gravel path, the figs were ripening along the wall above the kitchen garden, the air was sweet with fragrance . . ."

"I be fair homesick to hear ye tell it!" cried Goodwife Pitkin. "The very words do make my heart beat faster!"

Questions poured thick and fast.

"Eat they still manchets of fine white wheaten bread?"

asked Goodwife Rogers. "I did so love manchet bread. Here we eat brown bread, corn meal mixed with rye, or Indian bannock of corn meal only."

"Drink they still swish-swash in Essex, made of drained honeycombs and spice?" asked Goodwife Minching. " 'Twas good to cure the cough and ease the swallowing."

"Have ye been in fair London Town of late?" cried Mistress Hollingworth. "Saw ye the water-bearers? Heard ye the clop-clop of horses' hooves? The noisy street-cries: 'Hassocks for your pews,' 'Sweet lavender,' and 'Cherries ripe'?"

"Ay, ay, gossips!" laughed Widow Cummings. "To all I answer yes. Old England is Old England still, and ever will be!"

The women's eyes filled with tears.

Comfort's hands forgot to knit as she stared and listened.

"Heed thy knitting, daughter!" came the stern reproof from her mother.

Only Mistress Seward stood aloof and asked no questions. After a moment, she broke out: "Why come ye here, Mistress, to prate of the England we hope never to see again? Be ye wishful to make us homesick?"

Silence fell, as friendliness turned to bitterness.

"Homesickness be sinful to indulge in," cried Goody Lumpkin. "It be but weakness. Old England be best forgot."

The others, ashamed now of recent tears, joined in.

"Them that hunger after Old England fall into discontent and die," said Mistress Cartwright.

"Unless they take the scurvy first," added Goodwife

Minching in a tone of bitter sadness.

"To fix your eyes on Old England's chimney-pots bringeth on sickness, that we well know," sighed Mistress Hollingworth.

Widow Cummings rose to her feet, astonished. "But would ye then forget the land that bore thee, the land ye love so much?"

"Sister," reproved Goodwife Partridge hastily, "ye have done us a great unkindness to stir up our love for Old England, which we had thought dead. Speak of it no more."

Undisturbed, Widow Cummings opened a small bag and spread its contents on the table. Comfort's knitting fell to the floor as she ran forward to look.

"Gossips," said Widow Cummings quietly, "I brought thee seeds of herbs from my father's garden in Essex." She put small packets into the women's open palms. "Here's fennel to sharpen the eyes and the brain; rosemary to strengthen the memory; mustard to revive the spirits; lettuce to give peace and rest; borage to bring good cheer; and basil, sweet basil, to chase away sorrowfulness and melancholy. Of all these, I see ye have great need."

The women murmured shamefaced thanks.

Widow Cummings approached Goodwife Partridge. "These be London gloves, embroidered," she said, holding out three pairs. "I brought them for you, sister."

"Oh! Look ye!" "Ah . . . how lovely!" cried the women.

"Comfort!" scolded her mother. "Thy knitting. See ye to it."

The girl went back to her seat and took up her work.

"My hands be coarse and rough," said Goodwife Partridge, holding them out. "Not fitting for fine gloves."

"Here we work hard," murmured Goodwife Rogers.

"Here a woman must not be butter-fingered, sweet-toothed nor faint-hearted," put in Mistress Seward severely.

"For ten long years we've given no thought to gloves and finery," chimed in Goodwife Minching.

"Ye mean it well, sister," said Goodwife Partridge sadly. "But our clothes be old and shabby. Fine gloves become us not."

"Dear sister," cried Widow Cummings eagerly, "have ye forgot the fine apparel ye wore when ye were young?

Remember ye not the fair gown our mother wrought for thy marriage? With embroidered under-petticoat trimmed with silver lace, and great sleeves of taffety, three times slashed?"

"I see it still," said the Goodwife softly, while the women crowded close. "I mind yet the sweet rustle of its silken skirts. 'Twas in the sea-chest we threw overboard to lighten the cargo, on our voyage ten years ago. But we dare not speak of embroidered petticoats here. These gloves . . ."

"Our goodly Magistrate liketh not pride and vain-glory," said Goodwife Rogers.

"Parson Humphrey counselleth us to give our minds and hearts to higher things," said Mistress Seward. "He ever preacheth against intolerable pride in clothes and hair."

"Let me but show thee my mulberry London gown," cried Widow Cummings. "When thy goodly Magistrate and thy goodly Parson see it . . ."

"Oh, sister, wear it not abroad!" Goodwife Partridge's face turned pale. "This be not Old England. Things be different here, as ye will soon enough find out. It fares not well with those who follow after vanity. It betokens a carnal heart."

Goody Lumpkin, who had been standing by the door, now stalked out. "The words I have heard from this new-comer," she shouted back angrily, "be an abomination and a snare of the Devil. I will hear no more."

"She will tell it out abroad." The women shook their heads and whispered. "She is a tale-bearer."

"Are ye then afraid?" cried Widow Cummings boldly. "Why, what evil hath been done?"

After the women took their leave, Goodwife Partridge

handed the gloves back to her sister. "These I cannot wear. Nor can you."

"We shall see," said Charity with a smile. She turned to Comfort. "How goes thy knitting, lass? Let me pick up those stitches ye dropped." Comfort handed the stocking over.

The house was quiet after the women left. Thankful returned from the Minchings with a pail of milk. Goodwife Partridge went out the back door and soon returned.

"The gossips stayed full half the morn," she complained. "A waste of precious time. My work is but begun . . ."

"Dost carry thy own water, sister?" asked Charity, astonished.

"Ay!" said Goodwife Partridge, setting down her piggin.

"Ye carry water and do like drudgery?"

"I carry water, too," said Comfort proudly.

"So do I, though some time I spill!" added Thankful.

"Only the poorer sort do that in Old England," said Aunt Charity. "London tankard-bearers and country cottagers. The Indians, they help thee not?"

"They make not good servants," answered Goodwife Partridge. "A wild people they be, difficult to tame."

"I had bought the redemptioner from off the *Fearless,* had I known ye had no servant," said Charity thoughtfully.

"The wicked maid, Aunt? With sinful heart, who came off the boat *in her hair?*" Comfort's eyes opened wide.

"Ay, lass," replied Aunt Charity. "Kindness maketh a good servant of even a wicked girl."

Comfort pondered these words in silence. They sounded very strange. Goodwife Partridge filled a second piggin and brought it in. She set it on a form by the door.

"Why so much water?" asked her sister.

"We must have water for washing and brewing and cooking. We must have water to drink . . ."

"To drink? Drink ye then water?" asked Aunt Charity in surprise.

"We have little milk." Goodwife Partridge's tone was patient. "Our share is small. Three families, the Minchings, the Sewards and ourselves share the milk of one cow. God grant there be more, now that the *Fearless* hath brought more cattle. They be sorely needed."

"They be but thin and scrawny beasts," said Gaffer Partridge, who had just come in with the two boys. "And a winter of scanty feeding will not make much milk. Next summer, after they go out to pasture, perhaps we can hope for milk for all."

"We manage right well," added Goodwife Partridge cheerfully, "seeing every family or two hath a spring of sweet waters betwixt them, or the sea by their very door."

"Ye *drink* water?" asked Charity, unbelieving.

"Not salty sea water, but clear, clean spring water," answered her sister. "We have drunk naught else for so long . . ."

"Here, Aunt, take a drink!" Comfort filled a mug and held it to her lips.

Her aunt took a sip, then turned away with a wry face.

"It be not accounted a strange thing here, to drink water!" laughed Goodwife Partridge. "Ye must learn to like it."

"Here ye drink water and do without many delicacies enjoyed in Old England," said Gaffer Partridge solemnly, as he took a seat by the fireside. "Fountains do not stream forth wine and ale. Woods and rivers are not like butchers' shops or fishmongers' stalls. If thou canst not live without those things, the *Fearless* waits to take thee back whence thou camest. A proud heart, a dainty tooth and an idle hand be here intolerable!"

But Aunt Charity refused to be solemn. She turned to her sister's husband with a twinkle in her eye. "You *like* it then, John? You *like* water?"

Gaffer Partridge smiled. "I dare not prefer it before good beer as some have done," he said, "but any man would

choose it before bad beer, whey or buttermilk. It be far different from the water of Old England, being not so sharp, but of a fatter substance. It is thought there can be no better water in the world."

The children gathered round the fireplace.

"The Indians drink water freely," said Seaborn. "They take it up in their two palms and drink at the wrists."

"They drink naught but water," added Comfort. "Never any milk. They keep no cows."

"I gave Know-God a taste of my beer once," said Seaborn, chuckling, "and he spat it out like some vile thing!"

"Yet another sip of sweet water, Aunt?" asked Comfort, holding out the mug invitingly.

"No, no!" laughed Aunt Charity. "Take it away. But one sip for the first day. Life without Old England's ale will indeed be strange."

"We brew molasses beer," said her sister, "when we can get the malt from England."

"There be many new and strange things for each newcomer to learn," said Gaffer Partridge seriously. "A strange but fair land this."

" 'Tis said that those who commend it, do so in strawberry time or when wild roses fill the air with sweet fragrance," laughed Aunt Charity gaily. "But when the winter wind blows chill and bringeth hardship, they close tight their lips and say naught!"

"Despite all hardship, still we say the land is fair," said Gaffer Partridge. "Despite all we suffer, none wishes to return. There be but three serious inconveniences—Indians, wolves and mosquitoes. But these be naught beside that great benefit we came to enjoy—freedom to worship God as we please."

"Mos—kee—toes? What be they?" asked Aunt Charity.

"Creatures that have six legs and live like monsters altogether upon man's flesh!" laughed Gaffer Partridge. "The Governor saith that those who be too delicate to endure the biting of a mosquito should bide at home till they be mosquito-proof. Come summer, ye will make a mosquito's acquaintance and fall a-scratching like the rest of us, I doubt not."

Goodwife Partridge and the children laughed merrily.

"Be they worse than Indians?" asked Aunt Charity.

"Worse than Indians!" The family laughed again.

"Ye have Indians for neighbors?" asked Aunt Charity. "Is it safe then to go abroad?"

"None live in Fair Haven By-the-Sea," answered her sister, "save one, a boy, called Know-God. His family were taken by small-pox and he alone survived. English people brought him here four years ago and Parson Humphrey hath adopted him."

"Wherefore is he called Know-God?"

"When the Indians are put in mind of God, their usual answer is, 'we not know God.'"

"Know-God is fleet of foot and sharp of eye," said Seaborn.

"The Indians eat no salt, they live in mat-covered huts in the woods," explained Gaffer Partridge. "They live off the flesh of deer, bear, moose, raccoon, and fish when they can get naught else. They grow maize and eat *nokehick*—parched meal, powdered."

"They be dangerous?" asked Aunt Charity.

"They be friends when they be friendly," said Gaffer Partridge. "They be enemies when they be unfriendly."

"Your wild beasts be dangerous, too, be they not?" asked Aunt Charity. "I heard unearthly howling in the middle of the night, followed by the shot of a gun. What beast was it, come under my very window?"

No one answered. Aunt Charity looked round at the children's closed lips, then at her sister's.

"Why be ye then so silent? Sister, have ye forbidden the childer to speak? Think ye to spare me? Must not I know the worst soon or late?"

Still no one spoke.

"Comfort told me 'twas not a lion." She turned to her brother-in-law. "But surely I heard roars and loud wailing, as if wild lions came to life while man slept and took his rest."

Gaffer Partridge glanced at his wife, then answered with a bitter smile: "I took *not* my rest. Ye need not be affrighted of lions. 'Twas a sneaking wolf leaped over our paling fence and snatched a young goat from the pen. We lost the kid, but got the wolf."

"We feared to affright you," said Goodwife Partridge, "on your first night in this new land. I bade the childer hold their tongues."

The children now felt free to speak.

"Poor little kid," said Comfort sadly.

"T'other kid will be lonely," added Thankful.

"We have skinned the wolf already," boasted Seaborn. "His black hide hath great value among the Indians."

"The town pays fifteen shillings bounty as well," added Gaffer Partridge, "to help rid the settlement of the pest."

"We returned but now," piped up little Waitstill, "from hanging our wolf's head on the meeting house door. I will take you to see it tomorrow, Aunt. On the great stone step the blood drippeth red, in great puddles . . ."

"Ugh!" cried Aunt Charity, with distaste. "Mosquitoes, Indians, wolves! A strange land this!"

The children laughed.

CHAPTER THREE

Engines of Punishment

"**C**ome, sweet childer!" cried Aunt Charity. "The day is sunny and warm. We will go for a stroll. Methinks ye have sat still long enough."

Waitstill and Comfort came eagerly, but Thankful sat motionless beside God-be-thanked's cradle.

"I bide here to mind the babe," she said. "Mother is over-busy with the monthly washing. I like not to leave her."

"Thou art a goodly child," said Aunt Charity, patting her on the head. "Another day thy turn will come for a frolic."

"A frolic, Aunt?" asked Thankful soberly. "Better to spend one's days from early morn till set o' sun repenting of one's wickedness in the sight of God. Frolicking—there be no time for that."

"Hear the child preach!" laughed Aunt Charity. "Truly an old head on young shoulders . . ."

"Hush, sister, hush!" begged Goodwife Partridge, from the corner of the large hall, where her back was bent over a wooden tub.

"Ay, but I *shall* speak!" Charity's cheeks flushed pink. "Want ye then no children at all? Want ye to make sober old men and sad-faced women out of babes in their very cradles?"

"We try but to lead godly lives," said Goodwife Partridge severely.

"Come with me, childer!" cried Aunt Charity.

They started out briskly. Aunt Charity wore her London mulberry gown of soft kersey. Below the lace ruffles of the full sleeves, she wore her open-work London gloves. Her cut-work coif showed plainly under her black beaver hat, with its band of pearls. Comfort knew she had never seen anyone so beautiful.

"What ails ye, childer?" Aunt Charity looked down at the two sober-faced children. "Have ye forgot how to ope your mouths and speak? Do you never prattle, babble, cackle? Never frisk and skip about like young lambs? Be not so mannerly, I beg you!"

No words came. The lesson of keeping silence before their elders was well-learned.

"Let us find a high hill," said Aunt Charity, "where we can see naught but the blue sea—that little pond of water which separates us from Old England. I want to look across it and see dear England once more. I feel as if I've been away for years."

"We could pick bayberries," said Comfort shyly. "Black Cloud's squaw makes a useful salve by pressing them to powder . . ."

"But I promised I would take Aunt Charity to see the wolf's head on the meeting house door," interrupted Waitstill. He paused thoughtfully. "But if ye will be affrighted, Aunt, then 'tis best not to go."

"I shall not be affrighted, child," replied Aunt Charity. "I must learn all these new ways. I go with you to see the wolf's head."

"But it maketh me sick to see blood," cried Comfort, in distress.

"I be fair 'shamed of you!" scolded Waitstill. "Ye can wait then round the corner, while I show it to Aunt Charity. 'Twill not make thee sick to stomach, Aunt?"

"No, child," said Aunt Charity stoutly. "We go first to the hill, then to the meeting house. Tell me more about these Indians of yours."

"Ye have never seen an Indian, then?" laughed Waitstill.

"Of course she hasn't," replied Comfort. "Dark of skin and black of hair they be. They dress in deer-hide, tanned and fringed."

"Look ye now!" cried Waitstill. "There cometh Black Cloud and his squaw."

A tall Indian man, with a skin slung over one shoulder, appeared with his fat, dumpy squaw at his heels. The woman carried a load of beaver hides on her back.

"They be bound for the trading house, to barter their furs for needful supplies," explained Comfort.

Aunt Charity's eyes followed the pair. "Be they dangerous?"

"Not very," replied Comfort. "They come oft to our house. Black Cloud accounts himself my father's best friend, having once saved his life."

Walking on, they came to a broad stretch of bare hill, below the fort, where among scattering rocks, bayberries grew in silver clusters. Comfort gathered up her apron and the children ran happily about, picking. Aunt Charity stood silent and thoughtful, gazing across the open sea. Suddenly she realized the children were shouting. They *can* shout, after all, she thought to herself.

Then words smote her ear: "Run, Aunt, run! Make haste, Aunt, make haste!"

A moment of panic seized her, as she saw a herd of wild animals rush toward her. Over the rise of a great sand dune

they came, egged on by a shower of sharp stones thrown by a long-legged boy and a group of dark-skinned, scantily clad children. Aunt Charity gathered up her petticoats and ran with all speed. Comfort and Waitstill ran close beside her. Comfort's apron fell from her grasp and the bayberries scattered. In the shelter of a huge boulder they stopped and drew breath.

"Be they wolves?" cried Aunt Charity, trembling.

"Wolves!" laughed Waitstill. "Not wolves but swine. Know-God and the Indian children drive the swine off the beach—the tide be out."

The galloping hogs rushed madly across the rocky field, then down the hill, scattered helter-skelter among the narrow lanes of the village.

"The Indian women come to the beach at low tide to gather clams," explained Comfort. "Clams are a dainty with them for eating."

"The swine come too," added Waitstill. "They turn up clams with their snouts and eat them."

" 'Tis ever a fight between Indians and hogs," Comfort went on, "to see who gets the most clams."

"But why keep ye not your hogs in pens?" asked Aunt Charity.

"There be naught to feed them," replied Comfort. "They must forage for their own food."

"Wherefore they grow bold," added Waitstill. "The hogs rush up to eat when Mother throws her slops out by the door. They dig ditches in the streets and lie down and rest there when tired. They fight fiercely with dogs and chase people indoors."

"Hogs!" said Aunt Charity. "Yet another evil to contend with."

"Hogs?" cried Comfort. "We pay no heed to hogs . . ."

"Except to get out of their way!" added Aunt Charity, laughing.

"Now go we to the meeting house," announced Waitstill.

"Ay! To the meeting house!" replied Aunt Charity, taking his hand.

On the downward slope of the hill, they passed a rude shelter, a cave dug into the bank of earth, held up with wooden spars and a covering of turf. Not far away were

three crude hovels, their arched hickory framework covered over with rush mats or pine bark securely lashed. Each had a stone fireplace set at the end, with clay-daubed chimney.

"That one is called a dug-out," said Waitstill, pointing to the cave, "being dug out of the hill."

"The others be English wigwams," said Comfort.

Aunt Charity shuddered. "Do people live here?"

"The English men built them when first they came here to live," explained Comfort. "Now that we have better houses, with two rooms, a loft and thatched roofs, these be abandoned."

"But I see smoke coming from the chimneys," said Aunt Charity.

"Doubtless some of the newcomers from the *Fearless* live here till better houses be built," said Comfort.

Aunt Charity turned her eyes away.

The path followed the beach where the Indian women and children could be seen, unmolested now by swine, digging clams. The path wandered past the salt works where two salt-workers were evaporating salty sea water in shallow pans, and along by the fish flakes where rows of fish lay on wooden racks, spread out to dry in the sun. Then it came again to the village.

Aunt Charity looked about her. She saw the blacksmith shop with glowing forge, the brick works, and then facing the village green, two houses larger than the others, having two stories instead of one.

"That be the Magistrate's house," said Comfort, "and this the ordinary, Landlord Cluffe, proprietor."

" 'Tis called the Blue Anchor," said Waitstill. "There be

the anchor pictured on the sign."

"Have ye then no shops, no merchants?" asked Aunt Charity. "Is there then no place to buy?"

Waitstill shook his head. "Only the trading house," said Comfort.

A half-grown girl came swiftly up behind. She rushed forward and planted herself before them.

"Who art thou, lass?" asked Aunt Charity. "Why block ye my path?"

The girl wore no coif and her hair hung wild and loose. She was dressed in servant's garb, sad-colored gown of

linsey-woolsey, with kerchief and apron of calico. Her hand went to her bare head.

"My coif . . . I lost it, I ran so hard . . . to catch thee . . ."

"Who art thou? Why do ye molest me?" asked Aunt Charity again.

"Patience Tucker, if it please ye, Ma'am. Mind ye not Patty?" cried the girl. "Patience Tucker, ye redemptioner, whom ye 'friended on the *Fearless?*"

"Patty!" cried Aunt Charity, delighted. "I didn't know thee. So neat and clean and handsome ye look! Art well disposed? Good home, good mistress, food to eat, all else? A comfort 'tis to . . ."

"Nay, Ma'am!" Patty's voice was loud and coarse. "She beats me, Ma'am. I hate her. I came to tell ye, Ma'am. Take me away, Ma'am!"

"But, Patty, art trying hard, as ye promised, to be a good servant?"

"She beats me, Ma'am. I hate her, Ma'am, I'll run away . . ."

"Patience Tucker, listen ye to me!" Aunt Charity's voice was solemn and stern. "Ye gave me your word ye would be a dutiful servant, do as ye were bid . . ."

"She beats me, Ma'am! Oh, kind friend, if ye love me, take me away from her!"

"I cannot, Patty," replied Aunt Charity. "Those who are bound must obey. Your master and mistress have paid for your passage. You must repay them with five years' work. There is no other way. Go to your mistress and do your duty, or they will send you back to England sure."

The girl turned sorrowfully away.

"Come not abroad in your hair, Patty. Ye'd best find your coif and put it on, lest thy mistress chide thee," added Aunt Charity kindly.

"What a wicked, sinful girl . . ." began Comfort.

"Know ye why she is wicked, lass?" asked Aunt Charity. " 'Tis only because she has never known love."

The door of the ordinary opened and a tall man stepped out. He wore a steeple-crowned hat and a full black cape that switched about his knees. He paused, waiting till the group came up.

"The Magistrate, Aunt, 'tis the Magistrate!" Whispering, Comfort clutched her aunt's hand and pulled her back.

But Aunt Charity loosed her hold and advanced smiling.

"Widow Cummings, I believe," said the Magistrate.

Aunt Charity bowed her head a trifle.

"A topish hat, with a fair pearl hat-band, if I mistake not!" said the Magistrate, frowning.

"Ay, good sir! Pearl!" Widow Cummings lifted her chin.

The man's glance left the hat, descended downward, ignoring her bright eyes and flushed cheeks. "Thou hast whalebone in the bodice of thy gown, hast not?"

"Ay, good sir! Whalebone!"

His gaze continued downward. "Gown of mulberry kersey, is't not?"

"Ay, good sir! Mulberry kersey!" Aunt Charity smiled.

"And open-work London gloves?"

"Ay, good sir! Of the latest fashion!"

Down to the ground went the Magistrate's eyes. "Corked shoes, if I mistake not!"

"Ay, good sir!" laughed Aunt Charity gaily. "With woman's gear thou showest no mean acquaintance."

The Magistrate's face reddened.

"And if it please you, good sir," Aunt Charity went on, "I have come well-prepared for New England's biting winter. To keep my ears warm, I have a blue velvet hood!"

But the Magistrate saw no occasion for levity. He frowned and his voice was harsh. "I admonish you not only for flaunting unseemly apparel, but for boasting thereof. Pride and vain-glory—these be of Satan. I hereby warn you lest thy sins bring punishment upon thy head and dishonor upon thy God."

Widow Cummings lowered her eyes. "I should indeed be sorry, good sir, if such came to pass, for I am a godly woman," she said in a contrite voice. "I do but wear such apparel as I have formerly been wont to wear in Old England. This gown is one my mother bequeathed to me. She in turn, inherited it from her mother. The material is of the best quality, made to endure. If I should discard the apparel I brought with me from Old England, where may I obtain plainer clothing to replace it? You will perhaps direct me to the nearest shop and help me make a suitable selection?"

A group of people had collected. Among them, Widow Cummings recognized two of her first callers, Goodwives Minching and Lumpkin.

The Magistrate stammered uncertainly. "We have yet no shop . . ."

"No shop? How then can I buy?"

"The seamen ofttimes bring goods to sell . . ."

"Ay, I saw the cheap and shoddy pieces they brought on the *Fearless* and heard what exorbitant prices they asked," said Widow Cummings. "Is that the only merchandising you allow in your fair town?"

The Magistrate coughed. "There be shops in Boston Town . . ."

"And thirty miles to walk to get there," added Widow Cummings. "If then I cannot buy, perhaps I can find wool and have it spun and woven into a piece of enduring cloth?"

"We have only a few sheep," answered the Magistrate. "We expect more in the spring—but as yet no wool to sell. The Master weaver I sent for died on the voyage . . ."

"What then can I do?" asked Widow Cummings.

"Wear what you have, but see ye flaunt it not," growled the Magistrate. "For the flaunting of gaudy apparel, ye can be presented at Court. Take heed."

He stalked away angrily. The women passed by without a word. Aunt Charity took the two children by the hand and started to cross the village green.

"He liked not thy mulberry London gown," said Comfort sadly. " 'Twas just as Mother said. But I like it well, Aunt."

"And so do I," added Waitstill.

Aunt Charity did not trust herself to speak.

"There be the stocks!" cried Waitstill, pointing.

"And there the pillory and whipping post!" added Comfort. "They be engines of punishment for wrong-doers. Have they then stocks and whipping posts in Old England?"

"Ay!" replied Aunt Charity sadly. "In Old England there be wrong-doing too."

Soon they came to the meeting house at the opposite end of the green. It was a one-story building with a thatched roof and a row of five windows, fastened with strong batten shutters, on each side.

Comfort ran to the far corner to wait.

"Our wolf!" cried Waitstill, pointing proudly to the grim head hung on the blood-stained door.

Aunt Charity looked, for look she must to prove herself not faint-hearted. Then quickly she turned her eyes away.

"Come, childer, we go home now," she said quietly. "We have seen our wolf."

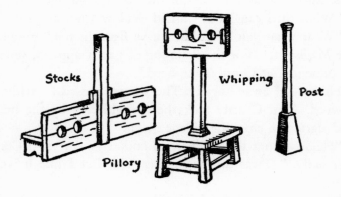

Stocks   Whipping   Post

Pillory

CHAPTER FOUR

Out from the Forest

The day was cold and blustery. A great fire burned on the Partridge hearth, sending bright sparks up the yawning chimney. Iron pots swung on chains and trammels, hung from the great green-wood lugpole which stretched from ledge to ledge.

Aunt Charity sat on the settle in the warm chimney corner with Comfort beside her. From the work-box on her
lap, she took out her needle and silver thimble. She began
to embroider cut-work on a strip of fine white Holland
cloth.

"What is't, Aunt?" asked Comfort.

"A new coif," said Aunt Charity. She slipped off her cap
and held the dainty white strip round her face. "Look ye!
Is't not handsome?"

"I like it well," said Comfort shyly. "Is't hard to do, the
cut-work?"

"Not when thy fingers have learnt mastery," said Aunt Charity.

"Could I then . . . could I have a cut-work coif?"

"Comfort!" called her mother suddenly from the lean-to at the rear. "Fetch here those river rushes. Don thy darkest green apron. Then come, scour the pewter well with sand."

The girl ran to do her mother's bidding.

Goodwife Partridge's words came faintly through the half-open door: "Think not of 'broidered coifs. Have I not told thee oft, daughter, that only a sinful heart longs after vanity?"

"Hath Aunt Charity then a sinful heart?"

The door went swiftly shut and Charity heard no more.

She went over her work thoughtfully, her needle flashing in the firelight. The outer door opened and she looked up with a start. There stood a dark-skinned, black-haired woman, dressed in deerskin clothing. The woman looked at her intently, then came forward and placed a carved maple bowl in her hands. Her seamed face broke into a broad smile, as she made a few strange sounds.

An Indian squaw! Charity's heart began to pound as she stared at the strange creature. She saw a girdle of blue and white beads about the woman's waist, bracelets on neck and arms, and links hung in her ears. Then she stared at the black eyes again. She tried to call for help, but no words came. She tried to get up and run, but she could not rise from her chair.

"Black Cloud take Knife Man's red coat," said the squaw. "Red coat no good in forest."

Charity's face turned white.

"He need net and fish-hooks and such toys," the squaw went on angrily. "Need pair of knives, and grindstone to keep them sharp. But he want Knife Man's red coat." She shook her head dismally as she squatted on the hearthstone.

Charity managed to rise. She made haste to the lean-to. "Indians . . . Indians . . ." she gasped.

"Be not affrighted," said her sister. " 'Tis only Black Cloud's squaw—come out from the forest."

"She talks of knives . . ." said Charity, trembling.

"Their word for English man is Knife Man," exclaimed Goodwife Partridge. "They never saw knives till the New English men came."

"She gave me this bowl," said Charity.

"Those dainty bowls they prize highly," commented her sister. "But such gifts come more from habit than friendship."

"Ye trust her not?" asked Charity.

"Ye heard what John said. When they be friends, they be friendly. But we must ever be on our guard, lest they turn over-night into enemies."

"She gave me this bowl," said Charity, rubbing its smooth sides lovingly. "She hath an honest look."

"Ay!" assented her sister. "Yet we can never be sure what they are thinking."

Goodwife Partridge came in and talked to the squaw.

"What said she? Is't English she speaketh?" asked Charity.

"A strange English, until your ears grow accustomed to it. Black Cloud hath given all his beaver furs in trade for an English man's red coat!" replied Goodwife Partridge, with a smile. "Small wonder she is cross. She says they came for needful tools instead."

"Hath she ever done you harm?" asked Charity.

"No, on the contrary, she hath helped us oft," replied her sister. "When first we came, she showed us where to gather wild foods in the woods, how to brew herbs and pound roots, how to make sweet-smelling and potent teas. She is accounted some sort of witch or doctor among her people, the Massachusetts Indians. She knows many cures."

"And yet you trust her not!" added Charity.

She sat down and resumed her embroidery. Now and then she lifted her scissors, which hung from her belt by a bright red ribbon, and snipped bits of cloth away. Good-wife Partridge brought her knitting and sat down beside her sister.

"Look ye and learn why I trust her not," cried Goodwife Partridge in a low voice. "Thy shining needle hath caught her eye. She looketh with envy upon thy bright scissors. Guard well thy needle and scissors, if ye want not to lose them."

"She would take them?" asked Aunt Charity.

"Ay! The Indians take whatever they can lay hands on. Light-fingered they be. We keep close watch always."

"But she hath an honest look . . ." Charity went on with her embroidery, now and then resting her glance on the woman.

Her scouring finished, Comfort replaced her soiled apron with a white one and came back to Aunt Charity's side. Thankful returned from the Minchings with the pail of milk. The boys came bouncing in, full of lively spirits, but upon the threshold changed at once into quiet, good-man-nered lads.

God-be-thanked toddled about the hall, his apron full of rye drop cakes fresh from the oven. He passed them out one by one with a solemn air. Unafraid he advanced to the In-dian squaw and placed a cake in her open palm.

The door opened and Black Cloud, dressed in his new red doublet, bow in hand and quiver on his back, came in. His face was dark and ugly, made more fearsome by tat-tooed designs upon his cheeks and a long lock of black hair hanging on one side of his head. Carved bone pendants in the shape of beasts dangled from his ears. Blue and white wampum beads hung round his neck and a girdle of the same encircled his waist. With a nod and a grunt, he squatted on the hearth beside Owl Woman, his squaw.

Goodwife Partridge continued her knitting and Charity her cut-work. Soon Gaffer Partridge returned. He spoke to the Indians, then sat down in a chair by the fire.

"Black Cloud sit in Lumpkin house," began the Indian. "Lumpkin squaw shout thunder words."

"Goody Lumpkin's been scolding her husband again," explained Goodwife Partridge. She turned to the Indian. "You eat dinner Lumpkin house, too?" she asked.

"No eat," said Black Cloud, shaking his head. "Lumpkin squaw not cook, she make big noise with her mouth. She shout loud to her man: Nannana Nannana Nannana Nan! Lumpkin one great fool to let her talk so. He not beat her good when she abuse him with her loud tongue. He say no word, he nimble of foot to run away. She chase Lumpkin out of house, she . . ."

"Chased you out, too?"

"She chase Black Cloud out too," he admitted.

The two women smiled.

Black Cloud saw the smile and rose slowly to his feet. Turning to Gaffer Partridge, he pointed his thumb at the two white women.

"Lazy squaws!" he snorted. "English man much fool, for spoiling good working creatures. Partridge much fool to let them sit in house with needles instead of digging in field."

Goodwife Partridge and Aunt Charity smiled.

"English man's ways be different," said Gaffer Partridge.

His outburst over, Black Cloud squatted down again.

The evening meal could not wait forever. Indians or no, they must eat. Luckily the potful of bean-porridge simmering over the fire was ample. Goodwife Partridge rose to her feet, stirred the mixture, then laid the table and brought out large flat loaves of brown bread.

"Soon we eat," said Waitstill, smiling. "Be ye hungry?"

"Ay!" nodded both the Indians.

Supper ready, the elders took their chairs and the children their places standing. Gaffer Partridge said Grace:

"O Lord, who givest thy creatures for our food,
Herbs, beasts, birds, fish and other gifts of thine,
Bless these thy gifts, that they may do us good,
And we may live, to praise thy name divine.
And when the time is come this life to end:
Vouchsafe our souls to heaven may ascend."

Comfort and Seaborn looked questioningly at their mother, who gave a slight nod. Comfort went to the dresser, brought two trenchers which her father filled with hot bean porridge, and took them to the Indians. Seaborn broke brown bread in pieces and thrust them into the Indians' hands. They ate greedily, with many grunts, then held out their trenchers for more.

"Didst get thy pair of knives, and grindstone to keep them sharp?" asked Seaborn.

Black Cloud growled and shook his head. Then he turned on his squaw and began scolding her in their own language.

Obediently she rose and left the house. He took out his pipe and began to smoke.

Charity looked at her sister.

"He telleth her to go home and work," explained Goodwife Partridge in a low voice. "So do they ever order their wives about."

"Will he never go?" asked Charity.

"Not till he's a mind to," answered Gaffer Partridge. "He's a lazy dog, he rests while Owl Woman works."

"Why not order him out if you want him not here?"

"We must keep friendship with the Indians at whatever cost," replied Gaffer Partridge. "Besides, I be forever in his debt. Once when Giles Pitkin and I were out on a hunting expedition, we lost our way in the wilderness. After wandering for two days we came on Black Cloud who led us to his lodging, fed our starving bodies and ministered to our sickness. After we were well again, he feasted us on the haunch of a fat bear. Then, in return for a fourpenny whittle (or fringed shawl), he conducted us through the unbeaten bushy ways for twenty miles, back home again. Ay! We be forever in his debt. I cannot order him out of my house." He paused, then added: "Let us give God thanks:

> *"O Lord our God, we yield thee praise,*
> *For this thy gracious store;*
> *Praying that we may have the grace*
> *To keep thy laws and lore.*
> *And when this life shall flit away,*
> *Grant us to live with Thee for aye."*

Comfort and Thankful made haste to stack the trenchers and scour them. Dusk had fallen and the room was in semi-darkness. Suddenly an unexpected noise came from the lean-to. A metal object of some kind fell to the floor with a noisy clatter.

"What is't? The billy-goat?" cried Seaborn anxiously.

"Mayhap 'tis another wolf," cried Waitstill, in excitement, "come now to eat up t'other kid! Make haste to shoot him, father, so we will have two wolf-heads hanging on the meeting house door!"

"Hush, son! Speak not!" scolded Gaffer John.

Comfort clutched God-be-thanked to her breast, and Thankful ran trembling to hide her face in her mother's apron. Goodwife Partridge's eyes never once left the crouching Indian on the hearth.

"Why, what fear ye?" cried Aunt Charity boldly. "Let's ope the door and see what 'tis!" She stepped briskly to the rear door and flung it open wide.

A strange scene met her eyes and the eyes of the family who crowded round—all but Goodwife Partridge, who kept close watch on Black Cloud. A brass kettle had fallen to the floor. It had fallen from a roof-hung shelf.

"What made the kettle fall?" cried Waitstill excitedly. The answer was plain. A bag of meal, lying now upon the floor, had pushed the empty kettle off the hanging shelf. There, scattered at their feet, sprawling out from the bag's open mouth lay a spreading circle of pale yellow corn meal.

"But what made the bag of meal fall down?" asked Waitstill.

Gaffer Partridge rushed to take his gun from its place over the mantel. Seaborn ran through the lean-to and out the back door. Soon he returned, pulling Black Cloud's sullen and angry squaw behind him.

"*Who* made the bag fall down?" shouted Seaborn angrily. "Owl Woman! 'Twas she who tried to steal our corn! I catched her just in time, ere she scuttled off to the forest. Look ye! Her back is covered with corn dust, her hair is covered too—the bag of meal fell full on her! Shall I not call the Constable?"

Black Cloud rose leisurely from the hearthstone and came out, followed by Goodwife Partridge.

"She stole our corn!" cried Waitstill, pointing.

"No, son!" said Gaffer John sharply. "She stole it not. The corn is still here. The brass kettle hath betrayed her."

"But what matters that? If the corn be still here 'tis through no fault of her own," cried Goodwife Partridge, whose patience was now at an end. "Have we not repaid these Indians with constant kindness? See what good comes thereof!"

Gaffer Partridge agreed. He spoke angrily to the squaw: "Ye tried to steal our corn, but the Lord hath found ye out! 'Twas the Lord who threw the brass kettle to the floor, to betray your wanton sin! Think ye, ye can conceal your wicked theft from the all-seeing eye of God?"

Black Cloud took up the accusation. "Beat her for stealing white man's corn," he cried. "Indians got plenty corn, not need to steal from white man, no. Beat her!"

Bewildered, Owl Woman looked about. Then her eyes rested on the strange new woman with the fair white skin. She ran to Aunt Charity, leaned over and kissed her hand.

"Wait a moment," said Aunt Charity. "I will have words with her. Comfort, come ye here, and tell me what she saith."

Charity, Comfort and the squaw went out by the paling fence. It was nearly dark now. After a few moments they returned.

"She says the English men's swine dug up the Indians' winter cache and ate much corn, which they had saved to eat in winter. She says Black Cloud bade her take corn from the English men, as much as the swine did eat. If she obey him not, he will beat her. He saith the corn rightfully belongs to the Indians—as much as the swine did eat. She speaks the truth. She is an honest woman."

When Aunt Charity finished, there was silence for a while, then Goodwife Partridge broke out: "That's like him! Deceitful, dishonest, not to be trusted . . . teaching her to do his thieving . . ."

"Shall I call the Constable?" cried Seaborn.

"Get you gone from my house, get you gone!" Gaffer Partridge shouted to the Indians in righteous anger.

"But, brother-in-the-law John!" cried Aunt Charity hastily. "Have you not told me we must keep friendship with the

Indians at whatever cost? Would you not sacrifice one bag of meal to keep such friendship? And have you not told me that Black Cloud saved thy life, fed thee when thou wast starving, brought thee to his home and nursed thy sickness? Dost now repay his good with evil, and order him from thy house?"

Gaffer Partridge's anger faded as suddenly as it came. He dropped his head in shame.

Then he walked over to Black Cloud and grasped him by both hands. "Friend!" he said. "Thou and thine are ever welcome to my house and to all that is therein. Ask ye for aught ye wish—even if it be corn—and it is yours."

CHAPTER FIVE

Day of Work and No Cheer

"What? Not keep Christmas?" asked Aunt Charity. "As I'm a God-fearing woman, what's this new world a-coming to?"

"No, we keep it not," said Goodwife Partridge sadly. "Life has been hard with us these ten years. It hath taken all our time and strength to feed and clothe our bodies—we've had none left for jollity."

"So sad-faced and dour you've all become!" Charity went on. "The moment I stepped ashore I thought you must all be a-mourning for summat, your countenances looked so heavy and sad. The childer—haven't they . . ."

Goodwife Partridge looked about at the little faces. She shook her head sadly as she spoke: "Seaborn was born on the ocean and the others here in this country. They know not the meaning of the word Christmas. The Governor, the Parson and the Magistrate say 'tis wrong. They say we came here for work and not for jollity."

" 'Tis time you heard it then, childer sweet!" laughed Aunt Charity. "Your Aunt hath come over the ocean to tell you of Christmas, sweet Christmas!"

"Oh, tell us, do tell us, Aunt!" begged the eager children.

"When thou hast been here for ten long years, thou wilt no longer laugh and tell merry tales," said Goodwife Partridge in a low voice.

" 'Tis time you heard of life in Old England, where mirth and jollity still reign, where life is not so stern—Dear Lord, may I never forget, no matter how old I grow. When the Christmas-time comes in Old England, dear-my-loves, 'tis the time when Jack Frost takes us all by the nose, so we make shift to rub out winter's cold by the fireside. 'Tis then the great Yule log is put on the fire, stories are told and songs are sung. And all the little boys and girls have puddings with raisins in them and minced pyes and Yule cakes rich and sweet . . ."

"But is it not wicked, Aunt?" asked Seaborn, pondering thoughtfully. "Parson Humphrey would say that such things are an abomination of heathendom and the ruination of souls."

"But oh, what fun!" cried Comfort, her eyes sparkling. "I should have liked it, had I been there."

Aunt Charity sat down on the bench before the fireplace and the children crowded close. It was a short time, but three months only, since this wondrous Aunt had come over from Old England with strange words in her mouth, strange words which were ever a temptation to hear. In the short time she had been here, the children had learned to love her dearly. Such tales as hers had never met their ears before nor set their hearts so eagerly fluttering.

"First of all the pewter and brass is polished so bright, it shineth like the sun indoors!" Aunt Charity's sweet voice went on. "The servants are washed and dressed in prettiest bib and tucker and here and there they run, as smug as new-licked puppies. For into the Great Hall all the Master's tenants and neighbors soon foregather to drink of his good ale, into which toasted Yule cakes are soaked and softened. The Yule candles are already alight when the mummers come to shout:

" *'A merry Christmas and a happy New Year,*
Your pockets full of money and your cellar full of cheer!' "

"Sister!" interrupted Goodwife Partridge severely. "Why remind us all of things which have gone past, never more

57

to return? Dost wish to breed discontent? Here we have more solemn things to engage the mind—work, the shortness of life, the swift-coming of death. I want not the children's heads befuddled. See how bright their eyes do shine, like in a feverish sickness, when one lieth at death's door!"

"Hush! Speak not of death!" Aunt Charity looked down at the children. "They are alive for the first time in years. 'Tis the first happiness they have known. The mere telling doth give them pleasure, their little lives have been so dark

and drab, so starved . . . Yes, ye have spent time and strength to feed and clothe their bodies, but their spirits ye have forgot."

She went on with her story: "The bouncing log on the chimney hearth doth glow like the cheeks of a country milkmaid. All the spits are sparkling, for the Hackin—a great sausage—must be boiled by daybreak . . ."

Gaffer Partridge suddenly entered the low-ceiled room. *"Hackin! Hackin!"* he cried sternly. "Who speaks of Hackin here?"

"I tell the sweet childer of Christmas-time in Old England, John!" answered Charity quietly.

"Christmas-time in Old England!" exclaimed Gaffer Partridge. "Is there still such a thing? I had forgot. I had forgot. Christmas! To think it still goes on as it did when I was young and ran about in pinafores. Here we have no time or place for such goings-on, but it can do no harm for the childer to know what once it was."

"Husband!" cried Goodwife Partridge in alarm. "Hast lost thy wits? How canst thou see thy children's heads befuddled by wild tales?"

Gaffer Partridge seemed not to hear his wife's words. He sank down heavily on the settle and stared into the fire. He spoke as if to himself alone: "I came but now from the village green. There saw I Goody Nichols chained to a post for scolding her man in a loud, harsh voice. William Muddleton was set in the pillory for idleness; and at the whipping post yonder, Constable Cartwright laid the cat-o'-nine-tails on a poor wretch's back, the while his cries did rend the air. Here in this fair land we seem to think of naught

else but wrong-doing. I like it not. Mirth and jollity we have forgotten quite. Is this the good life we came so far to find?"

"Oh, father!" cried the lass Comfort, running to his knee. "Did you keep Christmas too, when you were young like me?"

Gaffer Partridge turned away his head. The tears rolled down his cheeks one by one.

.   .   .   .

At daybreak on the twenty-fifth of December, two days later, no sound of caroling or of chimes broke the morning quiet. Now and then a chill breeze blew inward from the sea, bringing scattering gusts of snow. One by one the chimneys of the thatch-roofed cottages began to show thin trails of smoke.

Without, in the harbor, the frail ship *Fearless* still rocked at anchor. Salt-fish, clapboard and furs to a sufficient amount had not been assembled for her cargo, and the early closing-in of winter had prevented her return voyage across the Atlantic.

Through the narrow, winding path, on which a few months before the town cows had made their slow and patient way to pasture, walked Comfort Partridge with hood and shawl wrapped tight about her head and shoulders. In her cold, unmittened hand she carried a pail half-filled with fresh, froth-covered milk. As she hastened along toward her home, her little cowhide shoes made a sharp patter on the hard, frost-bitten ground. Suddenly she stood still and bent her ear to listen.

The Town Crier, stoop-shouldered and frowning, stepped round the corner. He rang his bell noisily, then in the pause which followed, cried out: "No Christmas! No Christmas!"

Christmas! All of Aunt Charity's words came tumbling back into the child's mind. She stood still and thoughtful, scarce heeding the little group of people who gathered to hear the Crier's words:

"Work to go on as usual . . . brick-making, blacksmithing, the chopping, riving and sawing of wood . . . townsmen to raise the new dwellings . . . women to spin in their doorways where they may be seen. A day of work and no cheer . . . a day of work and no cheer . . . by order of the Governor of the colony . . . to be enforced by the Magistrates . . ."

The listening people tightened their lips and went their way. Comfort shivered with the cold. A tear rolled slowly down her cheek. She grasped her pail more tightly and hastened home.

The heavy batten door swung slowly shut behind her. She put down her pail, removed her shawl and hung it on a wooden peg. Then she approached the table where the family waited—her parents and aunt seated on wooden stools and the children standing.

"Thou'rt late, daughter!" reproved Goodwife Partridge. "What delayed thee?"

"I stood for a moment . . . to listen to the Crier, Ma'am," answered Comfort. She pressed her white coif more firmly over her wayward curls, then straightened her white kerchief and apron. "The Crier said . . ." her thin voice pierced the silence, " 'at Christmas is a day of work and no cheer." Her blue lips trembled.

"And so 'tis!" echoed her mother. Then more sharply, "Hast forgot thy message? Didst inquire about Neighbor Minching and his sick wife? She's better—Goodwife Minching?"

Comfort Partridge shifted from one foot to the other. She was a responsible child. She had not lived her eight years in vain—eight years spent in learning not to forget.

"No, Ma'am, I forgot not," she replied slowly. "Goodwife Minching's taken a turn for the worse and Endurance is

come down with the sickness too. And the cow is 'most dry. This—'tis all the milk could be spared. Neighbor Minching asked if you and Aunt Charity could come and care for the goodwife, since Endurance must also keep to her bed."

"'In the midst of life we are in death!'" Goodwife Partridge gave her sister a meaningful look.

As soon as the porridge was eaten and the table board cleared, the two women left the house for their neighbor's. No one in the little seaport town ever called on neighbor in vain. Then Gaffer Partridge left, too, to help with the raising of a new pine cottage, one of those being built for the newcomers from the *Fearless*. And so the children were left alone.

It was when Comfort and Thankful were scrubbing the table board that they remembered.

"Just so do they do in Old England to make ready for the Christmas feast," said Comfort thoughtfully. "Aunt Charity said the board is always scrubbed till it shines as white as new-fallen snow."

"I wish we lived in Old England," said Thankful, biting her little red lip.

" 'Tis here we can worship God as we please," said Seaborn seriously. Being the eldest and a boy, he felt heavy upon his shoulders the responsibility of the younger ones. " 'Twas for that our parents came."

It seemed strange to hear the sound of children's voices. When their elders were present, they knew well to hold their peace and listen respectfully, speaking only when spoken to. Only when the elders were absent did their bright voices rise and fall freely like the piping of happy birds.

"I've seen laurel and ground-pine and hemlock greens a-growing in the woods," cried little Waitstill. "We need not go to Old England for them. They grow right here, even as our fuel grows at our very doors. We could fill our arms to over-flowing . . ."

"Why, so we could, my lambie!" answered Comfort, her eyes suddenly aglow. "Seaborn, let us keep Christmas just for ourselves this day—while the elders are away. 'Twill be a little play of our own and can do no harm. I mind all the things sweet Aunt Charity did tell."

Seaborn shook his head. "Parson Humphrey saith such things are an abomination . . ."

The door opened and Aunt Charity walked in.

"Your mother can do all that's needful for Goodwife Minching and her daughter," she announced. "She was worrited for fear God-be-thanked might fall in the fire and be burned or you'd forget to fetch wood enough and let the fire go out, so I thought best to return."

"Oh, Aunt Charity!" cried Comfort eagerly. "How good of you to come! We thought to keep Christmas this day, whether the Magistrate says so or no . . . just for ourselves at home . . ."

"Christmas! Good Yule!" said Aunt Charity softly. "I never thought I'd live to see it in this hard, cold, righteous land—but mayhap I will."

"There's Silence Pitkin—she's always sad and never talks or smiles," ventured Thankful timidly. "She would like Christmas, I know full well."

"And Preserved Rogers," added Waitstill. "He never plays stoolball for fear the Magistrate might pass and see him."

"And Temperance Seward," added Comfort, speaking more boldly now, "who always talks of death and thinks each day her last. We'll make things ready—the Yule log, a great feast, the Christmas greens—and bid them all welcome!"

"None of the other children know about Christmas," said Thankful shyly. "They have no sweet Aunt Charity to tell them."

" 'Tis time they knew," said her aunt. Her words were short, but a smile played on her lips. She set to work with a will and the children scurried about and helped.

"But what if the Magistrate comes?" asked Seaborn.

. . . .

At midday, when sad-faced Silence Pitkin and timid Preserved Rogers and solemn Temperance Seward and other little boys and girls came to the Partridge home, they saw many surprising things. They saw Christmas greens, laurel, hemlock and ground-pine wreathing the batten door and embowering the fireplace. They all helped drag the Yule log in to the hearth, the girls first washing their hands at

Aunt Charity's behest, in order, according to the old belief, to make the fire burn more brightly. They saw the shining board set with a feast and they ate heartily thereof—roast pork and codfish and mackerel, besides pumpkin sauce, beans and parsnips, and honey and maple sugar for sweets.

Afterwards came the games, *Blind Man's Buff, Puss in Corner, Hot Cockles, Forfeits, Shoeing the Wild Mare* and *Hoop and Hide.* Aunt Charity taught them all and none was slow in learning except little God-be-thanked who managed always to get in the way of the others, and Silence Pitkin who had sometimes to sit down for lack of breath, so unaccustomed was she to the playing of games.

Then Aunt Charity taught them a lusty carol and they all sang it together:

> *"Lo, now is come the joyful'st feast!*
> *Let every man be jolly,*
> *Each room with ivy leaves is drest,*
> *And every post with holly.*

> *Now all our neighbors' chimneys smoke,*
> *And Christmas blocks are burning;*
> *Their ovens they with baked meats choke,*
> *And all their spits are turning.*

> *Without the door let sorrow lie,*
> *And if, for cold, it hap to die,*
> *We'll bury't in a Christmas pye,*
> *And evermore be merry!"*

As the little voices rang out happily, Comfort noticed that her father and mother had returned and were standing back in the shadows watching. Then Preserved Rogers saw his parents and Silence Pitkin hers and before any one realized what had happened, the Partridge house was filled to overflowing with neighbors. The carol was sung over and over again and all the people smiled as they listened.

Suddenly a loud knock was heard on the batten door. The song died away and the children ran to their parents.

"What meaneth this frumpery?" A man's voice sounded in loud, cruel tones. Every one knew it was the Magistrate. His face was dark and flushed with anger as into the low-ceiled room he strode.

"What meaneth this?" he cried, pointing with his wooden cane. "What mean these greens about this hearth encircled?"

Little Waitstill had not lived long enough—but five years only—to learn that man can change a beautiful world into a sour one of his own making. In his innocence, he thought the strange, dark man had come not to berate, but to admire. He clapped his little hands eagerly.

"Oh, good sir!" he cried. "We found all the greens a-growing at our very doors. Dost not rejoice to see them? It seemeth as if the summer's sun hath changed the earth's white-furred gown into a gay, green mantle! Doth it not?"

"Hush, hush!" cried Goodwife Partridge in affright.

"Take the child with his noisy prattle away! Heard I not but now loud sounds of joyous singing and of mirth?" the Magistrate went on. "Methinks 'twas not the singing of holy Psalms!"

He bent his head and with his long nose, sniffed hither

and yon. "What odor greets my nostril? Smell I not sweet cakes, cakes made from forbidden sweetening and baked for Yule?"

The people fell back and not a word was said in reply.

"Ah! Ye need not speak. Me ye cannot deceive."

Angrily he pulled open the door of the Dutch oven still resting among the warm ashes on the hearth. "Baking Yule cakes, is that wherewith ye women waste your time? There . . ." but no, the oven was empty. "Ye've given them to your childer . . ." He looked, but he saw not a mouth that chewed, not a jaw that moved.

Only little God-be-thanked whimpered under the stern gaze. Then the babe's hand darted, swift as a bird, to his mouth and something was popped inside.

"There! A Yule cake! The child hath a Yule cake! Open thy jaws! Show me the cake!"

In a flash, God-be-thanked gulped once, then a second time and the cake was gone. Obediently he opened his mouth and there on his fat red tongue, a tell-tale line of white crumbs did show, which but angered the Magistrate the more.

He turned to the elders.

"Men!" he cried. "Where are thy tools? What hast thou done with axe, knife, auger, pit-saw, frow? Why be ye not at work? Know ye not we must build new homes for the newcomers from the *Fearless?*"

"Our tools are gone to be mended this day, good sir," spoke up one of their number.

"Women!" the Magistrate went on. "Why are thy spinning wheels idle? This is a day of work and no cheer."

"We have no flax, good sir," spoke up one of their number. "We cannot spin without flax."

"No tools! No flax!" snorted the Magistrate. He looked round the room and his eye lighted on the table board, from which the food and trenchers and pewter had been removed. It shone bright and white in the flickering firelight. "There! The shining board! That proveth there hath been Christmas-keeping here! The shining board . . ."

His eye lingered on it and as Mistress Charity watched him, she thought to herself that his face softened a little. Perhaps he too remembered Christmas in Old England, though he dared not confess it. Now, now was the time to speak. So Mistress Charity stepped bravely forth and told the Magistrate that it was she who had helped the children —the little children who had never known what Christmas was—to keep it.

" 'Tis the day of the Lord's birth!" she added softly. "He came to lighten men's hearts. In Old England, 'tis a day of joy and cheer. Joy and cheer are needed in this New England even as in the Old."

The Magistrate listened in amazement and as he listened, his frown grew heavier.

"Thou art frank, Mistress, and brave-spoken," he said. "Thou art new to this land, having but so recently stepped ashore from the *Fearless*. As time passes, thou wilt learn that our ways are not Old England's ways. We left them behind us to make a better life for ourselves here. Our law reads: Whosoever shall be found observing any such day as Christmas or the like, either by forbearing of labor, feasting or in any other way, shall be fined five shillings or be imprisoned. The edict is work or go to the gaol. But we suspend sentence this once, since thou art a newcomer. See ye, however, that it doth not happen again."

He opened the batten door. On the sill he turned. "Gaffer Partridge!" he called. "Remove this frumpery at once. See that this foolishness doth not happen again." He poked his wooden cane in the greens over the door and pulled them roughly down.

"Ay, good sir!" "Rightly, good sir!" "Thank ee, good sir!" obediently answered Gaffer Partridge and his neighbors.

The door closed and the Magistrate was gone. The men and women set to work at once pulling down the Christmas greens. While they worked, they looked at each other and smiled. "We kept Christmas once again—and with our childer, too!" There was a light in their eyes which had not been there before.

After they all went away Aunt Charity gathered the children about her and sat down on the settle.

"Was it wrong then, after all?" asked Seaborn.

"Oh, no!" answered Waitstill. "The greens were so beautiful to see!"

"And Silence Pitkin smiled again and again!" added Comfort. "She was happy for the first time in her life."

"And Preserved Rogers played games so lustily!" Waitstill went on. "We never thought he could play at all."

"And Temperance Seward spoke not once of dying!" added Thankful happily. "She asked if she could come back tomorrow."

"And God-be-thanked swallowed the last Yule cake in

the nick of time!" said Aunt Charity, with a laugh. "Well, dear-my-loves," she went on, as the tears filled her eyes, "ye've kept Christmas for one time only! Now hearken well —*That which ye have in your hearts can never be taken away!*"

"Christmas! Christmas!" echoed the children. "We've kept Christmas!"

"And ye'll never forget, will ye?" asked Aunt Charity.

"No, sweet Aunt!" answered the children. "Never shall we forget. That which we have in our hearts can never be taken away!"

WOODEN MUG and TRENCHER

PORRINGER

CHAPTER SIX

The Pewter Porringer

Waitstill stamped his feet and screamed. God-be-thanked rolled about on the floor wailing. Thankful flung herself on the bed and sobbed. The room was in an uproar. Comfort surveyed the scene and wondered what to do.

She looked at their visitor, who sat calmly on a block by the hearth. "Tell us no more," begged Comfort. "These tales the childer like not . . ."

Aunt Charity opened the parlor door, dressed in her cloak and French hood. She stared at the scene before her.

"Art come so soon, Aunt?" cried Comfort. "Hast done thy nursing? Silence Pitkin is better now of the winter sickness? Cometh Mother soon home from the Rogers'?"

But Aunt Charity did not answer. Her own questions came thick and fast: "What meaneth this bedlam? What hath happened here? Why scream ye and make loud cries?"

She fixed her eyes on the young girl who sat on the block and did not rise.

" 'Tis the Lumpkins' servant maid." Thankful jumped up from the bed to explain. "She hath come to tell us tales on a wintry day. Her head is bursting with tales of Old England."

"Mind ye not the maid who came with thee on the *Fearless?*" asked Comfort. "Goody Lumpkin hath sent her . . ."

The girl rose leisurely from her stool. "Patience Tucker, if it please ye, Ma'am!" She curtsied. "Mind ye not Patty whom ye 'friended on the long voyage?" She looked up with an engaging smile.

"I mind ye well, Patience Tucker," answered Aunt Charity slowly. "Ye look neat and clean and well-fed. But—why be ye here? Knoweth Goody Lumpkin ye be abroad? Have ye disobeyed her again?"

"No, Ma'am!" Patty shook her head vigorously. "My mistress bade me come borrow a porringer of yeast from Goodwife Partridge 'gainst her weekly baking on the morrow, and seeing Goodwife Partridge be not t' hum, I make free to talk to the childer." She put her arms round Aunt Charity's waist. "Such sweet childer they be, Ma'am! I love 'em to distraction. Such a fine, well-kept home, Ma'am. To live here and be your servant, Ma'am, would pleasure me right well."

Aunt Charity removed the girl's clinging arms.

"Why made ye the babes cry?" she demanded sternly. "What tellest thou them?"

"Right merry tales I telled," answered Patty gaily, "and yet they all fell a-weeping, such sillies they be! Hobble-de-gee, hobble-de-gee, I telled yon babe! I dandled him on my knee, I bounced him up and down, whiles I singed him a merry tune:

> '*First go the ladies, mim, mim, mim,*
> *Next come the gentlemen, trim, trim, trim,*
> *Last come the country clowns, gallop-a-trot!*' "

"Then down on the floor she dropped him with a thump," cried Thankful.

"And God-be-thanked screamed mightily," added Wait-still.

"But he hurted not his head, for he had on his Black Pudding!" laughed Comfort. She pointed to the wadded cap of black velvet. " 'Twas the same he wore on his head when first he began to go alone, to save it from bumps in falling."

"He hurted not his head, Ma'am. Could I help it he bawled fit to wake the dead?" asked Patty with a sly smile.

"Why tell ye wicked tales to the childer?" demanded Aunt Charity.

"Know ye not, Ma'am, it be Twelfth Night tonight?" asked Patty archly. "We did but play choosing of kings and queens in memory of the Three Kings of Old. I did but chant:

'Lavender's blue, diddle diddle!
Lavender's green;
When I am king, diddle diddle!
Ye shall be queen!'"

"What else?" asked Aunt Charity.

"I singed 'em Three Ships—they had not heard it afore
—and telled 'em fairy tales. Mind ye not how we talk of
fairies on Twelfth Night in Old England?"

"She telled us about the ugly devil," cried Waitstill. "He
hath horns in his head, fire in his mouth, eyes like red hot
coals, fangs like a dog, voice like a roaring lion, and tail
like a wolf, only ten times as long. I be feared to go outdoors lest I meet him."

Thankful went on: "She telled us of hobgoblins, witches,
ghosts and suchlike disturbers. She telled us of elves and
hags and hobgoblins. She hath seen spirits in shape of cows
and dogs and horses. She saith, when we hear a noise behind us, 'tis a spirit hiding."

Comfort nodded. "All this she telled us."

With set face, Aunt Charity approached the servant
maid. "Why come ye here, naughty wench, and tell such
tales?"

"Such tales be bracing!" answered Patty promptly. "They
make childer strong and obedient." She paused a moment,
then went on. "In Old England we tell such tales to childer
to make them afeared."

"Make them *afeared?*" cried Aunt Charity. "They sound,
indeed, like wicked servants' tales to me. Ye *want* to make
the childer afeared?"

"If they be afeared, then they will labor and be obedient to their parents." Patty Tucker fell a-weeping. The children stood round and stared at her.

"Ye be a wicked, thankless wench!" cried Aunt Charity, roused to anger. "These tales but make them fearful to go to bed; they make them to cry out when fast asleep; they bring on dangerous sickness. Is that what ye be after, Patty Tucker? A sad day 'twas for me when I first saw ye on the *Fearless*. Get ye gone from my sight!"

But Patty Tucker did not move.

Aunt Charity sat down and gathered the children about her.

"Remember this, dear-my-loves, fairies be *good* spirits," she said. "Twelfth Night is the time for careful observance of fairies, especially Robin Goodfellow, the dearest of them all. Good fairies love people and ever do them kindnesses. A bowl of water left in a clean room at night will attract well-wishing fairies. 'Tis Robin Goodfellow who comes to sweep or bake or thresh the corn for those who set a dish of cream and leave a clean hearth for him to lie on. Good Robin rewards thrifty housemaids by dropping money in their shoes while they sleep. But sluggish maids," she glanced at Patty, "he and his fairies pinch them as blue as a bilberry!"

"Will they pinch *her?*" asked Waitstill.

"Ay, if she be not a dutiful servant, and if she tell fearful tales . . ."

With a rush like a whirlwind, Patty Tucker flung herself upon Mistress Charity.

"Oh, Ma'am!" she cried. "Be not so harsh and unkind.

Ye be my only friend. Let me but come and live with you and I will serve thee well. I'll work my fingers to the bone for thee . . . if only ye'll forgive me and be my friend again." She fell sobbing on the floor.

"Patty Tucker! Get ye up on your feet!"

Patty rose.

"Take thy hankercher, blow thy nose and wipe thine eyes!"

Patty obeyed.

"Understand ye the harm ye've done, in affrighting the childer?"

"Ay, Ma'am!"

"Understand ye 'tis harmful to make them afeared?"

"Ay, Ma'am."

"Want ye to put them into a lingering sickness?"

"No, Ma'am."

"Be ye sorry for what ye've done?"

"Ay, Ma'am."

"If ye be truly sorry, then go ye home and prove it by being a dutiful servant to your mistress."

"Ay, Ma'am." Patty turned and left the room.

Aunt Charity followed her to the back door of the hall and opened it for her. A gust of wind blew in, chilling the room. She closed it quickly. She stood quietly a moment in the middle of the room, pondering.

The front door flew open, as if indeed Patty's spirits were abroad. It was not spirits, but Patty herself, returning.

"Oh, Ma'am!" she cried. "She'll beat me, she'll beat me!"

"Hast just run round the house, from back door to front, and come in again?" asked Aunt Charity.

"She cometh after me, Ma'am, she'll beat me, hide me quick!"

"Stand ye here by me," ordered Aunt Charity.

The door opened. Goodwife Partridge came in, followed by Goody Lumpkin and her friend, Goodwife Minching.

"Goody Lumpkin's redemptioner hath proved herself a vicious nuisance, given to idleness, disobedience, evil speeches," announced Goodwife Partridge, "and now she hath run away!"

"There she is, the wicked baggage!" cried Goody Lumpkin. "She hath neglected all her duties this day. Idle hussy, let me but quicken thy sluggishness!"

Goodwife Partridge looked from her sister to the girl.

"How came she here, sister? I telled Goody Lumpkin but now we knew her not, had never seen her, and that she hath never come to our house. She insisted the girl knew you . . ."

Patty Tucker hid behind Aunt Charity's full skirts. The children watched, crowding in at the parlor door, but did not enter.

"This maid came alone aboard the *Fearless*," explained Charity, "with none to help or guide her. I befriended her on the voyage. 'Tis but natural she should come to visit with one she knows for her friend."

"Make ye then *friends* with servants?" Goodwife Minching raised her eyebrows.

"I be ever a friend to a child in trouble," replied Aunt Charity softly.

"A child! In trouble!" sneered Goody Lumpkin. "Wicked, disobedient servant in need of a beating, ye'd better say." She pulled the struggling girl forth, letting loose upon her a flood of angry words:

"She hath run away and left her duties undone. In one corner I find a pile of bones, in another turnip parings, behind the door a heap of dust, under the table unwashed trenchers, in the cupboard the cat! When I ope the door, out jumped the beast, howling and scratching, fair in my face! When I scold her, justly, she doth throw a clog and hit me on the head. See ye the great lump? Then she runs away, and I search the town over. I had had the Constable and Tithingman on her trail, but for my goodness of heart."

"How now, Patty," cried Aunt Charity, in surprise. "This

tale agreeth not with thine. What was't ye came for? Ah, I remember now. Your Mistress sent ye to borrow a pewter porringer of yeast 'gainst her baking tomorrow. Show me thy porringer, so I may know thy tale is true."

"Porringer!" sniffed Goody Lumpkin. "But I bake *not* on the morrow! I said *naught* about porringer or yeast. I telled her if she deliberately make great lumps in the hasty pudding for spite . . ."

"Hold thy tongue, gossip!" said Goodwife Partridge sharply. "Thy constant scolding be enough to turn even the best servant's stomach. Show forth thy pewter porringer, wench."

Patty Tucker's eyes filled with tears. She hung her head and made no effort to bring forth a porringer.

Aunt Charity bent over her. "Show it me, lass," she begged. "Show me thy porringer and I will save thee a beating."

The girl cried harder. Aunt Charity turned to Comfort. "Hath she brought with her a pewter porringer? Hath she set it down somewheres about?"

"She spoke not of porringers, Aunt," replied Comfort. "She brought no porringer that I saw. Mayhap she carried it in her pocket."

Aunt Charity began a rapid search. She felt the girl's clothes all over, front and back. She patted her full skirts and there in the pocket felt a hard object of metal.

"No, no, no!" cried Patty, pulling away.

"Watch her, hold her tight! She'll run away again!" warned Goody Lumpkin. "When aroused, she can bite and fight like a wild-cat." She turned to Goodwife Minching. "Gossip, run ye with all speed. Fetch here the Constable!"

The door closed and the woman was gone.

"What is't in her pocket, sister?" asked Goodwife Partridge sternly.

Despite the girl's struggles, Charity brought forth the hard metal object and held it up. It was, in truth, a porringer.

Goody Lumpkin snatched it and stared. " 'Tis silver! All my porringers be pewter." She thrust it back. " 'Tis none o' mine. 'Tis much too fine for the likes o' me!"

Goodwife Partridge took the porringer. " 'Tis thine, sister —the silver porringer ye had as a child. Thy initials be here engraved. When we were children, we each had our own porringer. Mind ye not how they hung in a row over the hearth at home?"

"Widow Cummings' silver porringer!" cried Goody Lumpkin. "Patty Tucker brought no pewter porringer with her—not she! She came hither to steal a silver one!"

"Comfort, where found she Aunt Charity's porringer?" asked Goodwife Partridge.

Comfort came forward to explain. "She started to look in thy work-box, Aunt. It sat on Father's sea-chest by the window. I cautioned her not to. But she said one look would cure the fit of homesickness for Old England that brought on her such great melancholy, so I closed it and took it up to thy attic chamber. The porringer sat on the sea-chest, too, I think. When I came down again, I never noticed 'twas missing."

Patty Tucker stood near the door, with tears streaming down her face. Her thin shoulders were hunched together in dejection.

"She took it deliberately!" cried Goodwife Partridge. "She

invented the story of the yeast to gain entrance to my house
to do her wicked thieving."

"Surely now she is proved a thief!" cried Goody Lumpkin. "As soon as that slow-poke Constable comes, he will
clap her up in gaol!"

"Be not so sure," said Mistress Charity gently.

She thought quickly. The girl had nothing to love. She
had never had a bauble or a plaything or a gewgaw to call
her own. No wonder she coveted the bright shining porringer. How she herself had loved it when she was a girl!
Well, Patty should have it for her own. The best way to

win the girl over to honesty and well-doing was to be generous with her. Charity stood up straight and tall and her
cheeks flushed pink.

"Patty lass, come ye here." The tone of her voice meant
kindness and understanding, so, like a drooping flower turning toward sunlight, Patty came.

"Here is *thy* porringer, Patty!" Mistress Charity laid it
in the girl's outstretched hand. "I give it thee for a gift."

"Mine?" whispered Patty, her eyes wide with wonder.
"A gift?"

"Silver! 'Tis silver!" breathed Goody Lumpkin, in a tone
of awe.

No one spoke for a moment. Then Goodwife Minching rushed in with Constable Cartwright at her heels.

"How now? What's to do? Where's the thief? Fetch her here!" cried the man.

Mistress Charity faced him boldly. "Goodwife Minching hath been over-hasty, good sir. There was no need to call you. Patty is not a thief. She hath not stolen the porringer. I have given it to her. It is now hers to keep."

"But . . ." began Goodwife Minching, in astonishment.

"But . . ." began Goody Lumpkin. The two women could think of nothing to say. Such generosity was too great for their comprehension.

Constable Cartwright stalked out, muttering angrily.

"Take Patty home now, Gossip," said Mistress Charity. "I think ye will have a good and obedient servant. When she goeth astray, I suggest that instead of scolding, berating and beating, ye try kindness."

She picked up Patty's whittle from the chair and folded it gently round the girl's head and shoulders. The two women and the girl went out and the door closed behind them.

Comfort ran to her aunt. "Why did you give her the porringer, Aunt?"

"Because," said Aunt Charity, "she hath never had any one to love or trust her—in all her life. She hath never had any one to give her a gift. Poor Patty!"

CHAPTER SEVEN

From the Jaws
of Death

Comfort pushed her needle in and out carefully.
Now and then she stopped to thread it. "Think
ye 'twill be handsome, Thankful," she asked, "this
row of flowers, birds and fishes, when done in gay colors?"
"Ay!" said Thankful, glancing over. "But Mother liketh

it not. She frowned when Aunt Charity laid it out for ye. She said such colorful samplers smack of pride and vainglory."

" 'Tis but a way to learn useful stitches," protested Comfort. "Each row shows a new stitch—cross-stitch, tent-stitch, long and short stitch, crewel and feather stitch. After that, a row of cutwork, the same as on Aunt Charity's coif."

"Say not 'tis the stitches that pleasure ye," reproved Thankful, "but rather the wondrous pictures they make."

"Aunt saith, if I sew my sampler well, I may make a 'broidered bed-covering, such as people in Old England use to cover their great beds. 'Twill have roses and tiger-lilies, pinks, gilliflowers and forget-me-nots—all the sweets that run riot in English gardens. 'Twill have lambs and stags, lions and tigers, even men and women fashioned with beads for eyes and hair worked into tiny curls!"

Thankful turned away indifferent. "Sewing samplers maketh me weary," she said. "I like better some housewifely charge. I like better to pare turnips and pound corn—when turnips there be to pare and corn to pound. I like better to stir the pumpkin sauce." She went to the fireplace and took up the ladle.

Comfort's thread knotted and when she pulled, it became entangled. The narrow strip of linen was very long. She wondered if she would reach the end before she grew into an old, old woman. She put down her work and went to the lean-to to get wood for the fire. There she found Seaborn and Waitstill with the Indian boy.

"I gave Know-God my old knife," said Seaborn. " 'Twas lost for so long and rust-covered when I found it. He hath cleaned off the rust. Now he sharpens it."

Waitstill turned the grindstone while Know-God held the knife. His eyes glittered as he watched. He smiled as he tested the sharpness of the edge against his thumb.

The boys settled themselves on the floor. Know-God had taken off shoes, stockings and doublet. His legs and the upper part of his body were bare, but he did not seem to notice the cold.

"He maketh me a bow," added Seaborn. "A real Indian bow. He is grateful for the knife and wishes to repay me."

"What will you shoot?" asked Waitstill. "A wolf?"

"Ay, a wolf, if one cometh my way," said Seaborn. "But more likely a great fat turkey."

Comfort stood watching. "Where will you get arrows?" she asked.

"If he gives me none, I will make them myself," said Seaborn. "I know how the Indians make them. They take willow shoots and tie on heads of bone or stone sharpened to a fine point."

The Indian boy whittled patiently at the long straight sapling of hickory wood. Suddenly his hand slipped and the knife's sharp edge cut his finger to the bone. A stream of red blood spurted out.

"Oh!" cried Comfort. "Ye've hurted yourself."

Without flinching, the boy kept on with his cutting.

"Indians feel no pain," said Seaborn.

Know-God gave him a contemptuous look, but went on with his cutting. The half-whittled bow became spattered with blood.

"Or if they do," Seaborn added, "they show no sign."

"Oh, please let me bind it up," begged Comfort. She ran back into the hall and soon returned with a strip of clean white cloth.

But Know-God shook his head. He went out the back door, dug under the snow and found a tuft of grass. He pulled it up, rubbed the root over the wound, then bound the dead grassy top round the cut finger.

When the bow was finished and tightly strung with deer sinew, the two boys made ready to go outdoors.

"Where go ye?" asked Waitstill.

"Find arrows," said the Indian boy. "We go shoot."

"We will track turkeys in the snow," said Seaborn, "and bring home game to eat."

It was very quiet after the boys went away. God-be-thanked slept peacefully in the cradle. Thankful stood by the pot of pumpkin sauce and stirred without ceasing. Waitstill drew a chair to the window, knelt on its cushion and looked out.

Comfort took up her sampler again and pulled at its thread. It was hard to stitch on the sampler, with Aunt Charity away every day. The winter sickness, starting with the Minchings, had spread through the village. Silence Pitkin and her brothers had recovered, but now daily Goodwife Partridge went to the Rogers and Aunt Charity to the Sewards. Temperance Seward, just Comfort's age, was very ill. Sad-faced Temperance who talked so oft of death, lived now each day as if it were her last. Comfort's heart was filled with sorrow.

"It gladdens me to know that Aunt Charity sits with Temperance to cheer her," she said. Tears rolled down her cheeks.

"Weep not!" said Thankful. "We must all die. Nothing's so certain as death. If Temperance die, it be God's will."

"I be fair sick of pumpkin sauce," said Comfort, sniffing. "Naught to eat but pumpkin, morning, nooning and night. I like not the smell, I like not the taste. Sometimes I wish I might never see a pumpkin again."

"Ye be wicked then!" cried Thankful. "Heard ye not Parson Humphrey say the Lord feedeth his people on pumpkins till corn and cattle be increased?"

Waitstill turned from the window. "It slideth down easily," he said.

"I like not to live without bread or corn or milk," said Comfort. "Father breaketh the bread in such tiny bits . . ."

"To make it go farther, silly," said Thankful. "Waitstill, bring in more wood, or the fire will go out 'fore the sauce be cooked."

"I went but now to look," said Comfort. "The wood be all gone."

"Perhaps Father will soon return," said Thankful. "The men be in the woods chopping today."

"Green wood!" complained Comfort. "To fill the house with smoke."

"Smoke be good for catarrh and colds," said Thankful. "Father will bring all the green wood he can carry. Pray God we can keep the fire burning till then."

"Aunt Charity saith they eat roast beef in England," Comfort went on. "It tasteth summat like roast goat, only better. Even roast goat would taste good . . ."

"Hunger is the best sauce," said Thankful.

God-be-thanked woke and began to cry. Comfort picked him up from the cradle and dandled him on her knee.

"Cows, calves and goats be so scarce in the Colony, we cannot kill them," replied Thankful.

"Now that the winter's cold hath frozen up all the fish and game," said Comfort, "we must go empty . . ."

"Before we go empty," said Thankful, "we can dig up roots from the ground and pick up acorns in the forest."

"How can we dig in the frozen ground?" asked Comfort. "Know ye not the Indians have et all the acorns long ago?"

"Mayhap Seaborn will shoot a turkey," said Thankful, "or the Indians may bring us a gift of corn."

"They have no corn," cried Comfort, in vexation. "They eat acorns, I tell ye! And they come not to see us in winter. They roll up in blankets and sleep like bears in their dens. They wake not till spring cometh."

The room felt suddenly chilly. Comfort put God-be-thanked down on his feet to play with Waitstill. She pressed her hand over her empty stomach and thought of hot food. The combined load of grief, hunger and vexation seemed suddenly too great to bear.

"If only Aunt Charity were here," she cried, with tears in her eyes. "I cannot endure . . ."

"Wait ye in patience," said Thankful solemnly, "until deliverance comes. Wait ye in patience . . ."

The door opened and Aunt Charity entered. She had been away all night. Hollow-eyed and weary, she dropped into a chair and buried her face in her hands.

"How be Temperance?" Comfort scarce dared ask.

"Parson Humphrey hath been there these many hours," said Aunt Charity. "He prayeth God, if it be His will, to save her. He exorciseth the Devil and sendeth up prayers continually to God." She paused, then added in a low voice: "She lieth at death's door. She is given up by all. There is no hope."

Comfort, kneeling, dropped her head on her aunt's lap, and fell a-sobbing.

"Be she dead?" asked Waitstill.

Suddenly Seaborn burst in from the lean-to, with a huge wild turkey on his back.

"Now we go no longer empty," he cried. "The Lord sent a flock of turkeys direct in our pathway. See ye what I shot!"

Behind him came Know-God, a string of dead rabbits slung over his shoulder, his dark face smeared with blood. From the midst of the redness, his black eyes gleamed forth.

"O-o-o-o-h!" screamed Aunt Charity, in fright.

Then she recovered herself. " 'Tis but the Indian boy," she whispered. "I be tired and over-wrought. I first thought . . . 'twas the Devil himself come in human form . . . Parson Humphrey hath so filled my mind with thoughts of the wicked one. Mayhap God hath sent *him* for a sign . . . and not the Devil . . ."

She pondered thoughtfully. Seaborn talked of the hunt, but she heard not a word.

"Now we will feast on stewed rabbit and roast turkey," cried Thankful. "The Lord hath fed us in our emptiness."

Aunt Charity watched the boys unload the game, take water and wash. Then she spoke to the Indian boy and his answer was a vigorous nod.

"Oh, but, Aunt," cried Comfort, "ye cannot go. All the paths be choked with snow. The wind be shrill and harsh. The sun hath hid his face—more storms are coming. Ye know not the piercing cold of New England's icy winters, which freeze men's feet . . . and hands . . . and hearts . . ."

Thankful, too, cried out in protest: "Our mother would not let ye go. Ye know not the dangers which may beset you. No one goeth into the forest in winter, not even the men."

But Aunt Charity heeded not their warnings. "Ye will take me to Black Cloud's squaw?" she asked the Indian boy.

"Ay!" grunted Know-God.

Hastening to the loft, she opened her sea-chest and took out a silver spoon and placed it carefully inside her clothing. She put on her warmest doublet and petticoats, bound her French hood tightly to her head with scarves, and threw a heavy cloak about her shoulders.

"Shall I not go, instead of thee, Aunt?" asked Seaborn solemnly. "Tell me thine errand . . . why 'tis so urgent to see the squaw."

"Thou art fagged from thy hunt, lad," said Aunt Charity kindly. "The rabbits, the turkey—some one must clean and dress them . . . that they may be cooked, so we all may eat. See ye to it. Mind thy sisters and little brothers till thy parents return."

The door closed and she was gone.

Seaborn, Comfort and Thankful looked out the window and watched her walk in Know-God's footsteps. They saw the wind lash her skirts about her, they saw the two figures disappear from view, lost in the oncoming rush of snow.

. . . .

98

It was many hours later when Aunt Charity returned.

The children, who had fallen asleep in the chimney corner, rose stiff and chilled from the settle. The fire had gone out and the ashes were cold. Comfort rubbed the sleep from her eyes and stared.

It was like a dream.

There stood Aunt Charity, not tired, not frozen, not despairing. And there with her stood not Know-God, but Black Cloud's squaw, Owl Woman, blinking like an owl. Well-wrapped in many layers of skins, with the fur-side turned in, she wore round her neck a silver spoon tied to a red ribbon, and she carried in her hand a leather bag. Owl Woman smiled her broad smile. Aunt Charity smiled, too, as she handed out chunks of Indian bannock for all to eat. Corn! Where had it come from? How sweet it tasted on the tongue!

"Get ye to bed, deary-darlings," scolded Aunt Charity affectionately. "On the morrow, God willing, I bring you good news."

As they tumbled in, they heard the outer door close with a thump and knew that Aunt Charity and the squaw had gone out again into the wintry night. The nipping wind howled round the chimney, but the children, lost in sleep, heard nothing.

The next morning a huge fire blazed on the great hearth. Most of the wood was green, but Waitstill stood by ever-ready to feed it with dry twigs, to set it breathing again when it smoked. All the elders were at home, but Owl Woman did not appear. Aunt Charity kept to her bed and the children walked on tiptoe and talked in whispers. No mention was made of what had happened at the Sewards.

When Aunt Charity was up and about again, she spoke of her visit to the Indian village as if it had been but a lark. "Now can ye not say I know naught of thy neighbors, the Indians!" she boasted.

"Ye have proved yourself a brave woman," said Gaffer Partridge, "and not faint-hearted. Tell us then of your adventure."

"The Indian village was not where it was last summer," said Aunt Charity. "Know-God saith they often move them. One day it be here—many round, mat-covered huts with smoke rising from the smoke-holes. The next day it hath disappeared, with no sign left that ever it had been in that place."

"A good thing I tried not to lead ye," said Seaborn. "How then found ye the new location?"

"I had never found it, had not Know-God led the way," said Aunt Charity. "How *he* found it, whether by sight or scent or sound, only God knoweth! The lad was led of God. Truly he knoweth God."

"Found ye then Black Cloud's hut?" asked Goodwife Partridge.

"Not till after we had visited each hut in the village!" laughed Aunt Charity. "Ugh! What dirty, smoky holes they be to lie in. Each time we pushed aside the bear-skin, we bent double to enter the door. In some we saw as many as two-score men, women and children crouched, squatted, coiled up like hedgehogs, or lying on their backs with knees drawn up to keep their feet out of the fire. Dozens of dogs slept round them or walked, ran and jumped over them where they lay. Their fires they fed with fat pine-knots and, during the snowstorm, kept the smoke-hole covered up tight with mats, to keep out the wind."

"Ah, yes, so do they," said Gaffer Partridge.

"The air within was so dense, stifling and acrid," continued Aunt Charity, "it made one glad to get out in the roaring blizzard again. And oh, their barbarous singing— ay, they sing themselves to sleep!—how the noise hurted mine ears, swathed in many coverings though they were!" She laughed gaily.

"Where found ye then Owl Woman?" asked her sister again.

"In the last hut of all," said Aunt Charity. "She made ready her medicine bag and came at once. When I tied the silver spoon about her neck, I knew she would do aught I asked. But first she bade me lie down on a roll of skins and rest. She set a wooden bowl beside me and bade me eat. 'Twas fish and clams, ground-nuts and acorns, all boiled together. It looked a strange mess, but its taste was savory and it gave me strength."

"They have no corn then, to spare?" asked Gaffer Partridge.

101

"None," said Aunt Charity. "I made sure to ask. Their chief diet now be acorns, dried and powdered. They shared their last corn with me—the bannock I brought last night."

"Their ways of curing sickness be strange," said Goodwife Partridge. "In their noisy chants and mutterings, think ye they call upon the Devil?"

"God's ways be past finding out," replied Aunt Charity. "Can not then He use these tawny people as instruments to effect a cure? They live close to nature. They know all plants—their bark, roots, leaves and what use they be. They do but put into practice what they have learned."

Comfort could wait no longer. In the pause which followed, she broke out: "How then is Temperance? Hath she died and gone to Heaven's gate and ye not told me?"

"Praise God, she hath passed the crisis and is on the mend," answered Goodwife Partridge solemnly. "Your Aunt Charity hath snatched her from the jaws of Death."

"No, no! 'Twas not I!" protested Aunt Charity. "I know naught of sickness and cures—though I mean to learn. 'Twas Owl Woman."

Comfort took her aunt's hand in her own.

"She did it for love of you," she said softly.

CHAPTER EIGHT

Seven Stripes

Comfort Partridge ran happily along the path. The sun was warm for March and the frost was almost out of the ground. She skipped over mud puddles, stepping on tufts of grass to keep her shoes dry.

She sang a gay little tune. Spring had come again—the long hard winter was over at last. Summer would bring wild strawberries, blackberries, cherries, plums. It would bring fresh vegetables and herbs, a plentiful supply of corn, and milk to drink.

Suddenly a shadow crossed her path.

"Stop, lass!" Timothy Thatcher, tithing-man, stood before her. "I heard thee sing, I saw thee run, lass!" he said. "Whither goest thou?"

"On an errand for my mother, good sir," replied Comfort.

"Go not singing, whistling nor hollering along the street," scolded the Tithing-man. "Knowest thou not that running will scandalize good folk? Step out ahead of me now."

Comfort obeyed.

"Go ye now, soberly walking."

Comfort took a few short steps.

"Have ye then learnt thy catechism against the Sabbath Day?"

"Ay, good sir!" replied Comfort, halting. She leaned first on one foot, then on the other.

"Wag not to and fro!" ordered Thatcher. "How dost thou spend thy time? Is it in play and idleness with wicked children?"

"Nay, good sir."

"Let not play entice thee. Go ye now, but walk sedately," added Thatcher. "Stare not at every unusual person or thing which thou seest. I go now on a search, to see if there be any idle persons or profane swearers abroad this day." Turning down a side path, he left her.

Comfort heaved a great sigh. She came to Goody Lumpkin's house, whither her mother had sent her. Patty Tucker, the servant girl, sat resting on the front doorstep of the small two-room house.

"Thy mistress . . ." asked Comfort. "Be she not t'hum?"

"Nay," replied Patty, smiling broadly. "Nor my master, neither. 'Tis I, Patty Tucker, keep the house alone today."

"My mother hath sent me to ask Goody Lumpkin . . ." Patty Tucker put a strange object in her mouth and blew out her cheeks. Comfort stared. Then she finished her sentence: "Sent me to ask thy mistress would she let Aunt Charity teach thee to spin?"

"Teach *me* to spin?" cried Patty, in astonishment.

"It hath been ordered that children and others tending sheep or cattle should also be set to some other employment, such as spinning with the distaff, knitting or weaving tape," explained Comfort. "Aunt Charity thinketh thy mistress would wish thee to learn to spin."

"But I know how already!" cried Patty.

"Patty, ye don't!" cried Comfort. "Ye cannot spin nor weave nor knit. Ye told me so yourself."

"Well then, if I know not how, I need not do it," laughed Patty. "What ye don't know won't hurt ye."

Comfort stared at the strange thing in Patty's mouth. "What is't, Patty? Breathe ye then fire? I see smoke coming from thy mouth. Only the Devil breathes fire . . ."

"Ho, ho!" laughed Patty, taking her pipe from her mouth. "Be not such a silly. 'Tis but a pipe, with tobacco therein."

"To-bac-co? Tobacco?" echoed Comfort.

"The Indians grow it and smoke it to pleasure themselves," explained Patty. "The New English men smoke it too . . . mostly indoors . . . not when they go abroad . . . 'Tis forbidden to smoke in the street."

"Go ye in quickly, then," suggested Comfort, "lest ye be seen. I met Timothy Thatcher, tithing-man, in the path but now."

"That old snook?" cried Patty. "Always prying, peeping, strutting, snooping—like a nosey old woman so he is!"

"Speak not with disrespect of those in authority," said Comfort.

"What care I who sees me?" boasted Patty, taking another puff.

Lazily she emptied the slop-pail into a wooden trough by the door, removed her pipe from her mouth and called: "Sukey-sukey-suk'-suk'!"

Pigs came running from all directions and gobbled up the slops. Then they began sniffing for more.

"Their bellies be never full," sighed Patty, "like mine." She picked up a stick and began scratching the back of the thinnest and scrawniest pig.

"He's right tame," she said, between puffs. "Sometimes I

play he's my pet. Sometimes I take him in bed with me and he sleeps as nice and cozy as in a mud-hole." She laughed coarsely.

"In bed?" asked Comfort. "A dirty hog in your bed?"

"I washed him first in yon spring," explained Patty.

"In the spring wherefrom ye drink water?" asked Comfort.

Patty laughed. Several pigs had wandered into the house through the open door, but Patty paid no heed.

"Where be thy master and mistress?" asked Comfort.

"Gone to Thursday Lecture and good riddance," said Patty, with a broad smile.

"Ye be wicked to say such a thing . . ." began Comfort.

"I hate her," cried Patty. "She giveth me not enough to eat. Her bread is black and heavy and sour. Some day, when she vexeth me sore, I shall put a great toad in her kettle of milk."

A loud noise, first a clatter then a thump, came from the inside of the house. Patty ran in, with Comfort at her heels.

"Yon pigs will get their bellies full now!" screamed Patty, pointing her finger.

Comfort stared. The hearthstone was alive with pigs. A large iron pot lay on its side, flooding the hearth with an evil-smelling liquid, which spread rapidly over the floor. Snorting and grunting, the hogs began to guzzle it up.

"It maketh good hog-wash! Good swill!" shrilled Patty, doubling over with laughter. "The pigs be half-starved. They have climbed up on the pot and tip-tilted it over! Now they will get their fill for once!"

"What's the stuff in it, that smells so vile, Patty?" asked Comfort.

" 'Tis naught but wort," answered Patty, shrugging her shoulders. "I did what my mistress bade me. I set the pot off the fire when it was done a-boiling, so the mash could cool and sour."

"Wort for beer? Thy mistress breweth beer?"

"Ay, for the old man to drink!" answered Patty, laughing. "Now he won't have none!"

"Ay," said Comfort sorrowfully. " 'Tis all gone. What will thy mistress say when she finds out the pigs have drunk it up? Ye shouldn't let the pigs come in the house, Patty. A careless maid ye be. Thy mistress will beat thee sore."

"Dirty old pigs!" screamed Patty angrily. She picked up

a stick of wood from the hearth and started after them. Out the door and round the house she dashed.

" 'Twill do no good to chase the pigs and beat them, Patty," cried Comfort, following.

But Patty did not stop to listen. The pigs, well started now, dashed madly on, far ahead of even fleet-footed Patty.

"Stop!" cried Comfort, in distress. "Run not! 'Tis scand'lous, saith the Tithing-man. Patty Tucker, hear ye, walk sedately!"

But Patty did not stop or listen.

Down the hill and across the meadow ran the pigs. Across garden plots and front yards they scampered. Dogs scurried, goats leaped madly on their tethers, women gathered up their skirts to get out of the way. When they reached the village, the pigs slowed down.

The Thursday Lecture was just over and people were coming out of the meeting house. Lecture Day, known also as "a day of public shame," gave godly folk an opportunity to view the newest criminals, set up for an example in the public square. Today, Anthony Osgood sat in the stocks for taking fence rails from a neighbor's field and burning them for fuel. Not far away, Goodman Eliot hung his head in the pillory or "stretch-neck" for shooting a raccoon on the Sabbath.

But it was not at stocks or pillory that the people looked. They stared at the strange-acting pigs.

The pigs were moving curiously, waddling, tippling, staggering. Some stumbled over, then picked themselves up, only to fall over again. A few became vicious, nipping stray dogs and setting them yelping. Boys began to throw stones at the pigs.

In front of the Blue Anchor a horse was tied to a hitching post. It was a young, high-spirited bay mare. The pigs, plainly intoxicated now from their plentiful dose of Lumpkin beer, reeled round the horse, nipping at the animal's heels. The mare threw back her head with a jerk, snorted angrily and began to dance a jig.

The boys giggled. Patty Tucker stood with her arms akimbo and laughed aloud. Comfort could not keep her face straight. Then the assembled men and women broke out in hearty laughter. Drunken pigs were something new— not to be taken seriously.

A man dashed out of the ordinary, banging the door behind him. "Hold ye!" he shouted. "Who molests my horse?"

Rearing on its hind feet, the frightened animal threw back her head with a jerk, broke the halter and was about to prance away. The man seized hold of the strap and began to belabor the horse with a stout stick.

"Run away, will ye, my beauty?" he shouted. "I'll teach ye!"

Whack, whack, whack, he laid on blow after blow. The mare flattened her ears and bent her head, while her feet danced an unceasing jig.

"Hold now!" cried a booming voice. It was Jonathan Cartwright, the Constable, wearing steel cap and corslet, with a sword hanging by his side and a long black staff, tipped with brass, in his hand.

"I arrest ye, Master Dillingham, for transgressing our laws by inordinate cruelty to animals." He pointed to the welts on the horse's back. "Think ye to kill the beast in a fit of anger? We be in sore need of good horses in the Colony."

"Arrest me not!" protested Master Dillingham. "This hullabaloo be not of my making. Lock ye up the drunken pigs in thy gaol!" He pointed to the pigs who now lay huddled in a heap in the middle of the road, fast asleep.

"Drunken pigs!" cried the Constable. "Hast lost thy wits, man? Sleeping pigs, ye mean. What have sleeping pigs to do with thy sinful horse-beating?"

"They were drunk but now!" shouted Master Dillingham. "They did nip my horse by the heels and set her rearing. I did but lay on to prevent her running away. Would ye have so good a horse escape to the forest and turn wild?"

"Thou art drunk thyself," answered the Constable, "and not the pigs. Landlord Cluffe must be fined for selling thee too much liquor. Come ye then with me to see the Magistrate. Doubtless he will let thee sleep off thy drunkenness in yon gaol."

Hearing the commotion from his house across the green, the Magistrate lost no time but rushed to the scene. Constable Cartwright now fell silent, as the Magistrate looked about on the crowd, then spoke to Goodman Pettijohn, an innocent bystander.

"What meaneth this, a beaten horse, pigs sleeping in the middle of the road, people standing curious and idle?"

Goodman Pettijohn, puffed up by his sudden importance, cleared his throat. "It happened in this wise, good sir. I be busily occupied at my daily duties. Being a cooper, I be hammering pipe-staves to fashion them together into a barrel, when I hear a rushing as of mighty wings, like as a great storm, approach and pass my door. I do rub mine eyes to make sure it be not a heavenly visitation, when what do I see but a herd of swine dashing past, with two young maids, armed with sticks, at their heels. I rub mine eyes again to make certain I see aright, and there go the Lumpkin's servant maid with the eldest daughter of Goodman Partridge at her heels, the both of them together, running as if the Devil was a-chasing them . . ."

"Enough!" cried the Magistrate. "What hath this to do with Master Dillingham's beaten horse?"

A woman came rushing up. Comfort's heart quaked when she saw it was Goody Lumpkin.

"Patty Tucker! Ye rogue, ye baggage, ye scamp!" She shook the girl until her teeth chattered.

"In God's name!" swore the Magistrate. "What come ye here for, woman? How dare ye interrupt the course of the law?"

Goody Lumpkin burst out: "She hath let all the pigs run in my house, she hath spilt the wort for the beer and let the pigs drink it up, then she hath chased them all over town." She pointed toward the mud-hole. "There they be, my pigs, that I telled her to feed with swill and lock up in the pen."

"Drunk be they!" cried Goodman Pettijohn. "Staggering drunk!"

The crowd began to laugh again.

"See how they sleep it off!" added Master Dillingham, now aware of the humor in the situation.

"She is guilty of wilful disobedience! She must be whipped!" cried Goody Lumpkin. She turned to the Magistrate. "Saith not the law, good sir, that a disobedient servant shall be whipped? I have ordered her to lock ye pigs in the pen, so they run not abroad and terrify the populace. Hath she obeyed, good sir? See ye not the pigs far from my pen, sleeping now in the mud in front of the ordinary?"

"I see, I see, I see!" answered the Magistrate, considerably vexed. "Where be this serving maid? Fetch her here."

The Constable nabbed Patty Tucker by the arm and pulled her out to face the Magistrate.

"Be she the redemptioner brought hither by Captain Boswell?"

"Ay! the very one!" replied the Constable.

"I did but do my mistress' bidding!" cried Patty, tossing back her head. "Oh, good sir, whip me not!" She looked around wildly. Then, seeing a familiar face in the crowd, she cried out: "Save me, kind friend, save me!" But the Constable kept tight hold on her arm.

Widow Cummings hastened up.

Comfort ran and whispered in her aunt's ear, telling her what had happened. "I will see what I can do," said Aunt Charity in a low voice.

The Magistrate turned to Master Dillingham, the owner of the horse. "The law saith: 'We allow here no tyranny or cruelty towards any brute creature usually kept for man's use.' But seeing thou art a gentleman and hast had ample provocation, in that the drunken hogs did set on thy horse to drive it away, and ye did beat it, but to prevent such running away, therefore be ye for thy offense excused. As for the serving maid, who maketh such an uproar and setteth the whole town by its ear, she shall be whipt for rebellious carriage toward her mistress. Constable, lay ye seven stripes on her naked back!"

The Magistrate turned to Goody Lumpkin: "Woman," he said sternly, "had ye beaten this maid with more regularity, to impress upon her a lesson of horror of the public whipping post and the gallows, such public whipping would not now be necessary. Ye might have saved the Constable this painful duty."

"Oh, good sir, but I *do* beat her oft!" cried Goody Lumpkin. "I beat her when she sweepeth not the floor, I beat her when she sitteth idle, I beat her when she spilleth milk . . ."

"Hold thy noisy tongue, woman!" broke in the Magistrate. "A cleft-stick to silence it or the ducking-stool to cool thy hot temper awaiteth thee."

"How then will I get my pigs home again?" With this last squawk, Goody Lumpkin closed her mouth and slipped back into the crowd.

Widow Cummings now stepped forward.

"Be not so cruel, good sir!" she begged. "Brutality serveth no purpose. The maid hath been careless, 'tis true, but . . ."

"Widow Cummings," snorted the Magistrate, "hast thou come here then from Old England to take upon thyself the ordering of the Colony's affairs? Methinks thy over-frankness and plain-speaking will bring thee to no good end. If ye were clapt up for a while, mayhap ye would learn to use thy tongue less freely."

"I am a gentlewoman, good sir," said Widow Cummings. "Therefore am I at liberty to speak."

The Magistrate turned to the crowd. "Disperse your-selves!" he cried. "Get ye gone! Stand not here all the day idle! Constable, take ye the serving maid to yon whipping post!"

Widow Cummings placed herself in the Magistrate's path. "I would have a word with thee, good sir."

"Wilt tell me then perhaps," sneered the Magistrate,

"about the splendid bear-baiting and bull-baitings held in fair London Town, where cruelty to animals holdeth full sway?"

"Of such, I should be covered in shame to speak," answered Widow Cummings. "I justify not Old England's wrongs. No more do I justify *New* England's wrongs, such as I have here witnessed this day." She paused, then went on, while her eyes flashed angrily: "Ye allow no cruelty here, good sir, to any brute creature! Well and good! Whereas cruelty to children ye *encourage!* Ye spare your horses, but whip your children! So order *ye* your Colony's affairs!"

She flounced her skirt with an angry gesture and stepped out of the Magistrate's path.

The people, half-admiring and yet half-fearful of such audacity, moved away, following Patty Tucker, screaming and kicking, as she was led to the whipping post. Aunt Charity took Comfort by the hand and hastened off in the other direction.

"Come, lass! Make haste! We go home!"

But they could not hurry fast enough. The sound of the heavy lashes and Patty's loud screams fell like cruel blows on their ears, and brought hot tears pouring from their eyes.

CHAPTER NINE

An Ounce
of Mirth

"I will help thee," said Charity, "if you will save
out part of the fat."

"Fat?" asked Goodwife Partridge. "Why want
ye fat?"

"To make pancakes," said Charity. "Shrove Tuesday hath
come."

"Shrove Tuesday," replied her sister. "Fat Tuesday. I
had forgot. But such days have no meaning here."

"Remember ye not, sister, how in Old England all the housewife's stores of lard must be used up against the forty days of Lent? Remember ye not how our mother made use of the last of the fat?"

"She made pancakes for us all and for all the shroving children."

"Ye have *not* forgot!" chided Charity gently.

"I mind well how, as childer, we always went a-shroving," said Goodwife Partridge sadly. "But what good to think of that now? 'Tis of the past. Our ways be different here. I use up the fat, but not as ye think. I use up the fat to make cleansing soap."

"Soap!" Charity laughed. "Ay! In this new land, soap be more important than pancakes."

"All through the winter I have saved the refuse grease, as well as the wood-ashes from the fireplaces," explained Goodwife Partridge. "Water drained through a barrel of ashes maketh lye. Today I boil grease and lye together to make the soap. When done, 'tis like a soft, clean jelly. Next week I do the monthly washing."

"Have ye no time, sister, for pleasure?" asked Charity. "Must ye always work to the uttermost?"

"Idleness be the worst sin of all," replied Goodwife Partridge. "Time was given man by God to improve, not waste. An hour's idleness is a sin as base as an hour's drunkenness."

"At least then," laughed Charity gaily, "ye shall have pancakes for supper to cheer thee."

That afternoon Goodwife Partridge bent over a great iron pot which hung from a cross-bar rigged over a fire outdoors. The March wind blew in cold and raw from the open sea, but the glowing fire tempered the chill. Carefully she stirred the bubbling grease and lye from left to right.

As the soap began to boil, Goodwife Minching came up. "Good morrow, gossips!" said she.

After a word of greeting, Goodwife Partridge handed the soap ladle to her sister. "Wilt help?" she asked. "My poor back will break ere this day be over."

"Ugh! I like not this vile stench!" Charity tip-tilted her nose. "I like better the smell of sweet roses in the field."

Goodwife Minching frowned. "Life in a new country be not a bed of roses!" she said. "I hope ye will not take it ill, if I speak a word of admonition, Widow Cummings. Ye have done a great kindness in caring for us through our winter's sickness. Ye have served well the sick and needy through the long hard winter. Think me not ungrateful. But, be ye then so much better than the rest of us, that ye not only refuse to make soap but to smell it? Thou hast been here six months—time enough to learn that this be not Paradise, and to cease thy complaints."

"But, gossip, if our godly Governor delighteth his nose with the sweet fragrance of wild roses, may not I do the same?" Aunt Charity's voice was meek, but a twinkle gleamed in her eye.

Goodwife Minching took Goodwife Partridge hastily aside and spoke in her ear: "I look for a judgment from the Lord upon thy sister, if she mend not her ways."

"She meaneth well . . ." began Goodwife Partridge.

"She engageth in idle gadding and conversation, her fine apparel and vain example tend but to corrupt our youth. If she repent not her bold ways, our goodly Magistrate must perforce deal with her with a strong hand."

Her stern duty done, Goodwife Minching continued on her way.

Goodwife Partridge turned on her sister. "I be fair 'mazed at you, Charity!" she cried, with impatience. "To complain of the stench of soap before our good neighbor. My heart overfloweth with melancholy when ye be so light-minded. Thy foolish speech will do thee harm. Where be the childer? I hear them not."

"I sent them to the public square," said Aunt Charity. "Mistress Hollingworth sent word that one Master Gershom Flagg, merchant, hath come from Boston Town, to set up a shop in Fair Haven. I bade them look in his window and see what he hath to sell."

"Ye but fill their heads with vain-glory. I like it not," said Goodwife Partridge. "Now that spring is nigh and ships from England come again, Master Flagg will but offend the seamen."

"True!" agreed Aunt Charity. "He will but grow poorer, since the Magistrate hath decreed that no merchant shall buy poor and sell dear. Why then have a shop? A strange man this Magistrate of yours."

"A goodly man," said Goodwife Partridge, "though ofttimes over-zealous. He means but to see that all lead godly lives."

"Ay! He is so godly, he maketh other men want to be wicked!" laughed her sister.

"Charity!" scolded Goodwife Partridge. "I do rejoice the childer be not here to hear ye say such disrespectful words. Sometimes I know not whether ye joke or be serious. Here, stir ye the soap ere it boileth over. I would fain see if God-be-thanked be in mischief."

Aunt Charity grasped the great ladle, and with nose lifted high and head averted, began stirring slowly.

Goodwife Partridge paused on the doorstep. "No, no, stir t'other way! Always from left to right!" she called. "If ye stir the wrong way, 'twill spoil the soap."

As Charity began to stir in the opposite direction, a great wave of the seething mixture splashed over the side. It flooded the pot, ran down to the fire and caused a loud hissing. Her hand and arm were scalded from the hot steam.

Such work was loathsome. But she had learned to do many unpleasant duties since her arrival. She gritted her teeth and continued stirring. She looked down the winding path to see if the children were coming, but no one was in sight.

Goodwife Partridge came to relieve her. "If thou wilt sew God-be-thanked's pinafore, I will mind the soap. 'Tis a long, tedious task—this soap-making. It useth up one's store of patience."

Charity went indoors where God-be-thanked sat on the floor, playing quietly. After sewing the pinafore, she stirred the fire, hung a pot of fat on the hook, mixed up a batter and began frying pancakes. The room was soon filled with delicious fragrance. Now and then she opened the front window and looked out.

A great pile of pancakes lay heaped on a large trencher when she heard the sound of a bell in the distance.

"The Crier hath news of some sort!" she said to herself hastily. "Something hath taken place to delay the children."

But it was not the Town Crier.

Childish voices rang out, then the bell rang again. Far out over the window sill Charity leaned. A little procession came dancing up the path. Hastily she lifted the last pancakes from the deep fat and hung up her ladle. Then she flung wide the door and stood on the threshold.

" 'Tis the pancake bell! The pancake bell!" cried Waitstill, running ahead and waving a little bell up and down.

Aunt Charity rubbed her eyes to make sure she was not dreaming.

The little children came first, Waitstill, Silence Pitkin, Preserved Rogers, Rejoice Peabody, Mercy Hollingworth and others. Shyly they began to sing:

> *"A-shrovin', a-shrovin',*
> *I be come a-shrovin';*
> *A piece of bread,*
> *A piece of cheese,*
> *A bit of your fat bacon,*
> *Or a dish of dough-nuts*
> *All of your own makin'!"*

"Please to give us bread and cheese!" cried the children gaily, holding out their hands. "A penny, we want but a penny!" "Pancakes or dough-nuts if it please you, Ma'am!"

Quick tears came to Aunt Charity's eyes. She brushed them away and ran to fill the children's hands with the warm pancakes.

A stream of neighbors followed after the children.

"Pancakes!" cried Goodwife Rogers. " 'Tis Shrove Tuesday and I never thought to make pancakes! But I found a bite o' cheese to give the childer."

"All these ten year I have not once made a pancake," said Mistress Hollingworth, "yet the memory of them be sweet. A few pennies I found for the childer. How tuneful their childish voices, when 'tis not mournful psalms they sing."

"Oh, to think I should live to see a shroving once more!" Goodwife Pitkin cried happily. "I declare I'd quite forgot the rule for mixing pancakes."

Then Mistress Cartwright, the Constable's wife, appeared. "Who taught them to come a-shroving?" she demanded. "Let them have their fun, I say, while the men be away."

Goodwife Thatcher added, "Methinks this New England of ours be cold in more ways than one! Let them have their fun for once!"

Goodwife Partridge left her soap-kettle and hastened to her sister's side. "So now I see why ye made pancakes! Ye have taught the childer . . ."

"Not a word have I said," protested Charity, "about Shrovetide or pancakes. Not a word."

"How then do they know?"

Charity smiled. "Mayhap 'tis in their blood! God grant there be some things ye righteous Puritans cannot kill out, with frown and precept and punishment!"

"Sister!" reproved Goodwife Partridge. But there was no time now for serious admonition.

The women, meanwhile, had been tasting the pancakes. Goodwife Pitkin, finding the bowl still half full of batter, began dropping more cakes into the sizzling fat. Her happy face flushed red as she piled up another trencherful.

"Here, Mother!" cried Waitstill. "Taste ye a pancake for Shrove Tuesday."

Goodwife Partridge leaned over and let her small son feed her.

"Wheaten flour!" She turned on her sister.

"Wheaten flour! It reminds me of manchet bread!" cried Goodwife Rogers.

"Why, so 'tis!" cried the other women. "That's why the pancakes smell so savory and taste so toothsome! From whence cometh wheaten flour?"

Aunt Charity flushed. " 'Tis some I brought with me for the voyage in the *Fearless*. 'Twas packed in the bottom of my sea-chest. I saved it 'gainst a time it should be needful . . ."

"For Shrove Tuesday!" laughed the women happily. "Wheaten pancakes—how smooth and dainty like sweetmeats they be!"

Goodwife Partridge hastened back to her soap-making, but found it hard to keep her mind on the stirring. The little children had gone scampering off to the neighboring houses, singing their shroving song.

Now came the clang of a louder bell. The women flocked to the door to see another procession of older boys and girls. Among them were Comfort and Thankful, Temperance Seward, Thomas Tuck, Hate-Evil Eliot, Freedom Rogers and others. In the center walked Know-God, the Indian boy, carrying a cock tied on his bare back and a bell in his hand, which he rang lustily at intervals. All the others, loosely blindfolded, carried boughs with which they chased him about. Under pretense of striking at their leader, they managed to distribute their blows with stinging force on the gaping crowd which followed alongside.

"Ouch!" yelled old Goodman Jenney, skipping spryly out of the way.

"Lay on another!" cried aged Gaffer Wigglesworth. "This reminds me of the Constable and his cat-o'-nine-tails! Wow! How it stings!"

"Beat me! Beat me!" cried Patty Tucker, the redemptioner, dashing out from the crowd. "Bough-beating suiteth me better than the broom-beatings of my mistress."

"Heigh! Heigh!" "Lay on, lay on!" "What ho!" "Ouch, hurt me not!" came the cries as the little procession came closer.

"Pancakes! Shrove Tuesday pancakes!" cried the women, hurrying back into the Partridge house, some with broad smiles, others with tears in their eyes. Out they came with loaded trenchers, and everybody, young and old, set to work cramming and stuffing. Aunt Charity dug in her sea-chest again and brought out more wheaten flour. Goodwife Pitkin's face grew redder and redder, as she fried and fried. The supply of pancakes seemed inexhaustible. The little children, still singing, pranced back, ready for more. They all played together and happiness reigned.

"Who taught ye then to go a-shroving?" asked Aunt Charity.

The children crowded round her like bees round a honey-pot, knowing she loved them well. They looked at each other, wondering who should be the first to answer.

"Patty! Our Patty!" piped up Waitstill, who could wait still no longer. "Patty be like you, sweet Aunt Charity! Patty telleth us all the things they do in Old England!"

"Patty singeth us pretty songs!" cried Temperance Seward.

"Patty teacheth us pretty plays!" cried Preserved Rogers.

"Patty saith our faces be too long and sad, our voices too quiet and soft!" added Silence Pitkin.

"Patty wants us to be merry!" shouted Hate-Evil Eliot.

"Patty likes to hear us shout!" cried Freedom Rogers.

Patty, meanwhile, being unaccustomed to such lavish praise, hid shyly round the corner of the house.

"Patty Tucker, come ye here!" called Aunt Charity.

Patty put her head out. "Wilt reprove me? Wilt admonish? Wilt punish?"

Aunt Charity laughed. The children pulled the girl forward.

"Ye have made us all happy today, Patty!" said Aunt Charity.

"We thank thee, Patty!" "We love thee, Patty!" "Come, teach us new plays, Patty!" cried the children.

Patty stood still. Then she turned her head slowly and looked slyly over her shoulder. "But what if we be catched at our fun-making?"

With a very droll air did she say the words. The children broke out in riotous laughter. What a clown was Patty!

But Patty did not so much as smile.

For she saw Goody Lumpkin approaching, Goody Lumpkin, very cross and very angry. Patty watched her come and met her glance without flinching. She said under her breath, "This woman cannot hurt me!" Then when her mistress took her by the arm and dragged her homeward, scolding with noisy words, Patty smiled. She was still basking in the children's love and trust.

Standing by, the women saw and heard Goody Lumpkin. They watched her drag Patty Tucker away. For a little while Patty had seemed the incarnation of childhood. Now she was a disobedient servant again. The women shook their heads. "The day will come when that woman will fry in her own grease," said one.

Then they roused themselves. "What if the sin-searchers return?" they asked. "The Magistrate, the Constable, the tithing-men?" They looked over their shoulders in fear.

"They be perambulating the bounds this day, thank the Lord!" said Mistress Hollingworth, with a half-hearted laugh. "They are not apt to return before sun-setting."

"So do they in Old England—remember ye not?" said Mistress Charity, "each year between Easter and Whitsuntide. The men go in a great procession to renew landmarks, to cut deeper the blazes on the trees, to pile up heaps of stones or plant new trees for new landmarks, to straighten out all uncertain or disputed boundaries."

"Our men take with them the most trustworthy of our youth," added Mistress Cartwright, "so that when they be grown to manhood, they will remember the boundaries as laid out."

"Hath Seaborn gone with his father?" asked Goodwife Rogers.

"Ay!" replied Goodwife Partridge proudly. "A steadfast lad he, to remember." She paused and listened to the sound of the children's happy voices. So unusual it was, it brought quick tears to her eyes. As she bent over to stir the thickening soap, fear suddenly smote her.

Dropping the ladle she cried out: "Sister, ye do wrong to encourage this laughter and gaiety! It becometh not children of godly parents. Better for them to repeat their Catechism and sing holy psalms, 'gainst the coming of the last day!"

Charity picked up the ladle and stirred. "Remember ye not when we played games as children," she said softly, "how ye called me 'Madcap' and I called ye 'Mischief'? An ounce of mirth—one little ounce—is worth a pound of sorrow. Ye spoke this morn of feeling sadness. A merry hearth doeth good like medicine. The laughter and gaiety of little children be ever a good cure for melancholy. A light heart lives long . . ."

Goodwife Partridge clapt her apron over her head and sobbed.

"But I will send them away now, sister, if their laughter offend thee," added Charity gently. "Childer! Sweet childer! Go ye home now quietly."

"Ay! They'd best go!" echoed Mistress Cartwright, " 'fore my husband gets sight of them. Make haste, childer, lest ye be seen and punished."

Goodwife Thatcher, the Tithing-man's wife, threw up her hands. "If my man was to see such goings-on," she exclaimed, "he'd not sleep a wink for a week, he's that godly!"

"And if the Magistrate got one glimpse of such madness, he'd clap us all up in gaol," added Goodwife Rogers.

"Go ye home, childer," repeated Aunt Charity, "ere thy one happy day be spoiled."

Taking their children by the hands, the women led them slowly homeward. "Shrove Tuesday and pancakes!" they whispered. "Never now will ye forget!"

CHAPTER TEN

On a Fair May Morning

The wrinkle-faced squaw waited outside. Know-God was with her.

"Gather ye up all the baskets, childer," said Aunt Charity. "We will bring home greens and roots and herbs."

"Be this a pleasure jaunt to the wilderness?" asked Goodwife Partridge.

"No, sister," answered Charity. "Owl Woman hath promised to show me all good things that grow in the forest. She will teach me some of her cures for sickness, against the coming of winter."

"But the childer? Need they go frolicking?" asked Goodwife Partridge.

" 'Tis the first warm day we have had," replied Charity. "Winter hangeth on over-long, and spring cometh late in this strange land. In Old England, the primroses bloomed weeks ago . . ."

"But why need the childer frolic?"

"To celebrate the coming of spring, the coming of flowery May, if ye wish to know," said Aunt Charity with spirit, "lest their little souls freeze up with cold."

"Speak not of pagan feasts," scolded Goodwife Partridge. "Such days and seasons be here unlawful, and displeasing to the Lord. Ye have grown over-bold since Shrovetide."

"God grant I be ever over-bold," said Aunt Charity.

"Goodwives Lumpkin and Minching have spread the word abroad and all the men have been told what happened here that day," said Goodwife Partridge. "Ye have not heard the end of it yet."

"I make no secret of aught I do," said Aunt Charity, with set face. "Though the fields have eyes and the woods have ears, I take the childer a-maying—all those who wish to go. 'Tis no occasion for shame or secrecy but for joy."

The children ran and brought their friends. Where Aunt Charity went, they all would follow. So along came Temperance Seward who talked no more of death, Silence Pitkin who had learned to sing and shout, Preserved Rogers who loved lustily to play, Freedom Rogers who strove to learn the meaning of his name, Know-God Humphrey, whose wild spirit none could tame—all these and others. A gay and happy throng trooped to the woods that fair May morning, led by the Indian squaw and Aunt Charity.

Spring had come on so quickly, it seemed strange to see no hard-frozen ground, no sun-thawed puddles of mud, no dry dead leaves and grass. But in their place marshes and fields alive with fresh green, trees sparkling with warm red buds and tender new leaves. Instead of the cold raw winds from the sea, the air blew soft and sweet, laden with the scent of hawthorn, dogwood and wild cherry.

The path led across the meadows, beyond the common cow pasture and out toward the forest. Soon they came to a leafy grove, half shadow and half sunlight, alive with blooming flowers.

With cries of happiness and shrieks of laughter, the children fell upon the flowers and began picking. So many kinds there were—violets, trilliums, jack-in-the-pulpits, adder's tongue, lady slippers and small sweet-scented pink blossoms hidden away under dry, dead leaves.

"Here be Parson Humphrey preaching a sermon!" cried Waitstill, holding up a jack-in-the-pulpit.

"Here be the sweetest mayflowers of all!" cried Thankful, her small hand filled to over-flowing with arbutus. "Mayflowers—we will ever call them mayflowers, because they bloom in May."

Owl Woman pointed out all the wild flowers that would

fill the summer air with fragrance—sassafras, musk roses, balm, laurel and bush honeysuckle. She pointed out berry bushes which would soon bear fruit—gooseberries, bilberries, raspberries, treacleberries, hurtleberries and currants. She pointed out the herbs suitable for meat and medicine—sweet marjoram, purslaine, sorrel, pennyroyal, yarrow, myrtle, saxifarilla and bayes. She called attention to the tangle of wild grape vines swinging from the tree-tops, looping and swaying from one tree to the next, festooned now with fragrant blossoms. She told of the wondrous fruit which would ripen in the harvest moon.

The two women, Indian and white, walked slowly. Now and then they stopped to touch a leaf or dig a root. They talked of the seasons when each plant was ripe for gathering or digging. They talked of brewing and steeping and other modes of preparing. They talked of many sicknesses and the cures for each. In spite of the difference in background and upbringing, they spoke the same language and understood each other.

Meanwhile, Comfort had wandered off alone, her hands full of flowers and over-flowing. But always just a step away, she saw more—larger and of a brighter hue.

"Go not too far!" A branch rustled and a quiet voice spoke. She looked up to see that Know-God had followed her.

"Snakes!" he warned. "With rattles in their tails!"

"Snakes come here where flowers bloom?" asked Comfort.

The Indian boy nodded his head.

"I be not afeared," said Comfort.

Know-God pulled a root from his pocket and held it out. "Snake-weed," he said. "To eat as soon as stung."

Comfort picked more flowers while he watched.

"Come back!" warned the Indian boy again. "Wild beasts here."

"I saw a rabbit but now," laughed Comfort, "go hopping over the mayflowers. A chipmunk came up to eat a nut from my hand, a partridge fluttered down close beside me, and a flying-squirrel leaped over my head. I be not afeared!"

"Come back!" warned the boy again. "Indians here."

"Indians!" cried Comfort. "Black Cloud's squaw, yes. She is our friend. Her people, the Massachusetts Indians, they be all our friends."

"Bad Indians!" grunted Know-God.

"Ay!" laughed Comfort. "Ye think the Indians bad, since ye have become an English boy."

"Me not English boy," growled Know-God. "Me not know English man's God."

" 'Tis good Parson Humphrey hears you not," warned Comfort. "No doubt he would punish you for such wicked words. Be you not grateful he saved you from the small-pox?"

Know-God frowned as if displeased and walked away.

The woods were darker now, with no sunshine sifting through, and the shade was pleasantly cool. Suddenly a red fox darted across an opening and disappeared beneath thick underbrush. The odor of pine needles, hemlocks and sweet fern was strong in the dampness. An owl hooted, then came a rustling of something breaking through the undergrowth behind her.

Comfort rose quickly to her feet. Was it Know-God back again?

Suddenly a loud whoop rang out, which sent a cold chill down her spine. Her flowers dropped to the ground. Was it a war-whoop? Bad Indians! What did Know-God mean by that? Her father had said that Indians were friends when they were friendly, but one never knew when they might turn into enemies.

Then she saw Know-God dashing toward her through the brush, his black eyes gleaming with excitement and fear. Uncouth words poured from his mouth and his arms were waving wildly.

Comfort looked behind her. A huge black animal stood high over her, holding out both its arms, as if ready to embrace her. It looked at her with small, beady eyes.

The next instant Know-God grabbed her by both arms and dragged her roughly to one side. He pulled her with all his strength and thrust her into a hollow between two near-by boulders. She looked up just in time to see the great bulky black form of a bear slog past. Behind ran Know-God, armed with bushy branches. More whoops rang out, and a number of young Indian braves came into view and gave chase.

Comfort's heart pounded in her bodice and her breath came quick. As soon as the bear and Indians were out of sight, she rose from her hiding-place and ran back to find the other children. She ran first this way, then that, but the woods seemed always to grow denser and blacker, and she knew not which way to go.

Then Know-God appeared again at her side.

"Who were the braves?" asked Comfort. "Bad Indians?"

"Braves of Josias, nephew of Cutshamakin, sachem," answered Know-God. He walked soberly on ahead. She followed at his heels.

"A bear!" she cried, as she came up. "Know-God hath saved me from a great black bear!"

Beside a cooling spring, Aunt Charity, Owl Woman and the children were resting. They listened in astonishment, as Comfort told her story.

"So bold he stood there," said she, "his arms outstretched as if . . ."

"He would give thee a bear-hug!" added Preserved Rogers.

"He did but love thee, lass!" laughed Aunt Charity.

"Ugh!" cried Comfort, in distaste. "Some bears be over-friendly."

"Would I had been there!" cried Aunt Charity. "I've seen no bear since I went to a bear-baiting in London Town long ago."

"A bear-baiting! What was't, Aunt? Tell us!" cried the children.

Aunt Charity's face saddened. "There be always some people who love to laugh at others' sufferings, animal or human," she replied. "Some are callous to the sufferings of beasts or think they suffer not at all. For sport, they greatly delight to fasten a bear to a stake, then set great English bull-dogs to worry and tease it. The poor bear defendeth himself against the angry dogs, biting, clawing, roaring, until at length he sinks down, defeated, in death. I never went but once. Bear-baitings be cruel, wrong and unjust—forever a blot on Old England."

The children looked at each other and were silent.

"The Indian boy hath been led of God to save thee, Comfort," said Aunt Charity. "To both we owe our thanks." She looked at Know-God who sat by himself a short distance off. "Come ye now, rest and eat."

Beside the tumbling brook the children ate brown bread and cheese, and drank of the sparkling waters. Owl Woman ate, too, then took her leave and waddled back to the Indian village.

"I speak now of more pleasant things," began Aunt Charity. "I will tell thee how the English children spend May Day."

"Oh, tell us, Aunt, tell us!" begged the children.

"On just such a fair May Day as this in Old England, the children rise before the dawn and, led by sweet music and the blowing of horns, walk out in the meadows and the green wood. Oh, how they rejoice their spirits with the beauty and savor of sweet flowers, praising God in their hearts for His goodness and love. They frisk and dance about like young lambkins, they break down green sycamore branches and hawthorn boughs, and adorn them with pretty nosegays and crowns of flowers.

"At sun-rising they return, all flushed and happy and care-free. They deck all the doors and porches with greenery, then they set up on the village green a tall pole, called a Maypole . . ."

"A Maypole?" cried Temperance Seward. "A tree with blossoms? How pretty!"

"A tall, straight pole," said Aunt Charity. "This Maypole they deck with garlands and ribbons of bright colors, and they spend the day a-dancing round it. Their feet be light as the wind, their faces bright as the sun, their hearts gay as the birds. Hand in hand the happy children dance, round and round the Maypole, twining their flowery garlands and colorful ribbons!"

"A Maypole! A Maypole!" cried Silence Pitkin and Thankful Partridge. "We would love a Maypole too."

"Why cannot we have a Maypole?" cried little Waitstill. He ran to pick up the branch of a tree.

"We could play May-games here, in New England, just as our fathers and mothers were wont to do in Old England," cried Comfort.

"Is it summat like going a-shroving?" asked little Mercy Hollingworth. "'A-shrovin', a-shrovin' . . .'"

Comfort watched her aunt's face and saw a shadow fall upon it. She knew it was a shadow of uncertainty and doubt. Then the shadow faded and her aunt's face brightened.

"May Day! May-games in New England!" said Aunt Charity softly. "So ye shall. 'Tis part of your heritage. So who be I to deny you?"

Stranger things never happened in Fair Haven By-the-Sea than on that pleasant day in May.

Back to town with a long straight pole the children came, a pole felled and trimmed by Know-God, the Indian boy. Back to town came the children armed with flowery baskets, blossoming boughs and gay-colored garlands.

First they set baskets of flowers at the doors of the houses, then they wreathed boughs and greenery around doors and windows. Aunt Charity brought out from her sea-chest a great abundance of gay-colored ribbons. These they tied to the Maypole, set up in a place of honor on the green in the public square. Then they danced round it, singing and shouting, making up songs of happiness and praise, giving thanks for all the beauties of springtime.

Their parents came out, rejoiced to see them so happy, and to listen to their songs:

> *"Come lasses and lads,*
> *Get leave of your dads*
> *And away to the Maypole hie,*
> *For every fair*
> *Has a sweetheart there,*
> *And the fiddler's standing by.*
>
> *For Willie shall dance with Jane,*
> *And Johnny has got his Joan,*
> *To trip it, trip it, trip it, trip it,*
> *Trip it up and down,*
> *To trip it, trip it, trip it, trip it,*
> *Trip it up and down."*

Know-God sat at the base of the pole and watched.

It was there that Parson Humphrey found him. Parson Humphrey was a spare man, thin and tall. His face was lean and creased with wrinkles. His eyes had an earnest, anxious look, becoming to one who bore upon his shoulders the spiritual welfare of the town.

"Why sit ye idle here, my son?" he asked. "Satan loveth an idle dawdler. Wait ye for him?" His voice held dignity and yet defeat, as if he knew in his heart this Indian lad could never be a son to him.

The dancing stopped and the children crowded round, faces red and flustered, caps and hats awry, eyes beaming bright.

"He saved *her* from the bear!" cried Waitstill. The children pointed at Comfort Partridge.

"Her? Who? What bear?" stammered the Parson, taken

by surprise. "You did run away again, my son, to grieve me?"

The Indian boy looked at the ground and did not answer.

Comfort spoke up. "I did but walk in the forest alone, when a great bear rose up before me. Ere he could take me in his great arms and squeeze me . . ."

"He wanted to give her a bear-hug!" cried Preserved Rogers.

"A warm, sweet bear-hug!" echoed Mercy Hollingworth.

"Such levity becomes . . ." began Parson Humphrey.

"Hush, children, hush!" cried Aunt Charity. " 'Tis true, good sir. The Indian boy hath been led of God to accompany us and save Comfort Partridge from the clutch of the wild beast." She went on to tell the whole story.

"A crowd of young Indian braves chased the bear away, good sir," added Comfort.

"Come here, my son," said the Parson. The boy came and stood before him. "It gladdens my heart to hear this. Ye have won the hearty thanks of all in the village. God hath filled thy heart with grace." He turned to Widow Cummings.

"But why have ye been to the forest, Mistress?" he asked, wrinkling his anxious brow. "Methinks wild beasts and Indians be not fit company for gentlewomen and little children."

"We went to search out roots and herbs, with the help of Black Cloud's squaw," explained Aunt Charity. "For our protection, Know-God consented to accompany us. Well hath he done his duty this day."

The people began talking and laughing again.

Then out from the Magistrate's house and across the green came a group of grave men in broad white collars and steeple-crowned hats. It was the Magistrate himself and four tithing-men, who had been receiving instructions on how to more zealously guard the morals of the people, each the ten families under his charge.

"Let us run before he sees us!" whispered some of the children.

But Aunt Charity said boldly, "We make no secret of aught we do. We be not cowards!" So the children crowded close around her.

Parson Humphrey explained briefly about the bear. The Magistrate stared at the Maypole, at the draggling streamers and the flowery garlands, now sadly wilted. He looked round upon the gathered company and centered his stern gaze upon Widow Cummings and the clustered children.

Then he turned to the tithing-men.

"Which one of you hath the Partridge household under his charge?" he demanded.

Timothy Thatcher timidly stepped forward. "Me . . . I have . . . good sir!"

The Magistrate frowned.

"Saw ye not this company of revellers rise in the early dawn and scamper off to the woods?"

"No, no, good sir! I slept soundly in my bed, good sir. I saw them not," answered Thatcher.

"Saw ye the bear and made ye an effort to shoot it?"

"No, no, good sir! My gun be rusty, I have yet molded no bullets . . ."

"Heard ye not the singing of May-songs and the playing of May-games?"

"No, no, good sir! I heard naught, I saw naught—the doors and windows of thy house from whence I came but now be tightly closed. Besides I was engaged in prayer . . ."

Impatient and angry at the man's foolishness, the Magistrate turned from him. He faced Widow Cummings.

"I have been patient with you, Mistress, but this time ye have gone too far." He bit off his words sharply. "We celebrate here in New England no pagan feasts. First, ye teach the childer how to keep Christmas; then with them ye go a-shroving, and now ye go a-maying! Truly Satan walketh about, *fair of face and in fine apparel,* seeking to ensnare our youth. We now have many counts against ye. See that ye present yourself at the next meeting of the town Court. If ye obey not, Tithing-man Thatcher will lead thee, with Constable Cartwright's help."

Aunt Charity hung her head for a moment. Then she saw the children whose arms clung round her waist, whose hands pressed tightly her own.

"I will come, good sir!" she said. She lifted her chin and smiled.

Early plow

CHAPTER ELEVEN

Ever=present Danger

"Seaborn, wake ye!" called Gaffer Partridge. "The sun riseth."

Comfort heard her brother stumble, half-asleep, out of the house.

"Blah! Bla—a—ah!" sounded his horn. Again and again

she heard the sound which brought children forth from their beds and sent them to the barns to turn the cows loose.

With spring had come the need of a cow-keeper. Seaborn had been chosen for this responsible office by the family tithing-man. He rose at break of day and, gun over shoulder, drove the town cows out to the common pasture. There he kept a sharp lookout for wild beasts and enemy Indians. Before sunset, he brought the cows back to their barns again.

"Comfort! Comfort!" called Goodwife Partridge.

As sleepy as Seaborn, Comfort washed and dressed herself.

"Thy father hath gone to the field to plant corn," said her mother. "Go quickly and milk the goat. We be in need of milk for breakfast." She handed her a piggin.

Goodwife Partridge had but laid the table board across the trestles when a loud scream rang out. She seized the gun and rushed to the dooryard.

Comfort stood still, terrified. There lay the milking stool overset, a puddle of goat's milk on the ground, and a paling loosened from the fence—but no goat. Goodwife Partridge ran to the fence. It was not yet daylight, but she saw a dark form slinking away dragging the goat behind it.

"A wolf!" gasped Comfort. "He snatched the goat from under my very eyes!" She followed her mother back into the house, fell on the settle and sobbed. " 'Twas a black wolf with glaring eyes and glistening fangs! He oped his jaws wide enough to gulp the goat in one bite."

Aunt Charity came running. "There, there, deary-

darling," she soothed. "Speak not of the wolf. Come now and eat thy breakfast."

Goodwife Partridge filled the children's porringers with hot porridge, but there was no milk. A trencherful of fresh fish, which Aunt Charity had broiled over the hot coals, sat in the middle of the table. The children helped themselves to fish and brown bread with their fingers. But Comfort could not eat. Hearing footsteps come round the house, she trembled.

"Who cometh at break o' day?" asked Goodwife Partridge.

Timothy Thatcher, tithing-man, appeared in the doorway. Comfort stared at him and tried to recollect her catechism. Thoughts of disobedience, Sabbath-breaking, unseemly running and other crimes darted through her mind. Had she been guilty of aught?

"Peace to this household!" announced Timothy Thatcher. "Peace . . ." He scratched his head to remember what to say next. "Be the Widow Cummings to home?"

"Ay, good sir!" said Aunt Charity, coming forward.

"Suffer the evil-doer . . . to be brought out from his hiding place . . ." stammered Thatcher. " 'Tis my duty to admonish . . ."

"Thank you, kind sir," said Widow Cummings.

"Ye think me kind, then?" cried Thatcher, beaming.

"Ay, good sir, exceeding kind," replied Widow Cummings. "Ye would not hurt a bee, or a fly, or yet kill a mos-kee-to!"

"Wouldn't I then! Bang!" He slapped his hands together and roared loudly. Then he recovered himself, resumed his dignity and went on: "Thy conduct, Mistress, hath caused no little scandal in this fair town. 'Tis my duty to admonish thee . . . to tell thee that immoderate rioting and unseemly revelry be not allowed . . . that evil-doers be not tolerated but be hauled up before the Magistrate and be either clapped into gaol or warned out of town . . ." He stopped to draw breath.

"Why, Mistress," he cried, "the people talk of naught else since May Day but how ye set up a Maypole under the Magistrate's very nose and teached the childer May-games and dancing! 'Twas a wondrous sight to see! I mind how

when I was but a lad in Old England, how I jumped and
kicked up my heels . . ." He stopped abruptly and scratched
his head. Then he began again: "I be come to admonish
. . . and see that ye . . ."

"Appear at the next meeting of the town Court," added
Widow Cummings with a smile. "When will that be?"

"In good time . . . in good time . . . I will inform thee."
Tithing-man Thatcher left the house as suddenly as he
came.

To Comfort's surprise, Aunt Charity was unusually cheerful all the morning, but she herself felt loaded down with
sorrow.

Towards mid-day, Goodwife Partridge called Comfort
to her. "Carry ye this dinner to the field for thy father's
nooning."

"But I be afeared of the wolf!" cried Comfort. "The wolf
be abroad!"

"Nonsense!" replied her mother. "Indulge not in foolish
fears. Go ye, tell thy father what hath happened to our she-
goat. Go ye also to the pasture and take Seaborn his dinner.
In the midst of life, we be in ever-present danger. Trust ye
in God and rest content."

Comfort took the kerchief-tied bundles and started out.
The air was warm and balmy. A gentle breeze shook her
red shag petticoat as she trudged along. Soon she came to
the newly-plowed field. Ridges of black soil lay overlapping
each other, in long rows. The rows curled over the brow of
a hill and were lost to sight.

Goodman Rogers had unhitched his horse from his
wooden plow, and stood now in the shade of a tree, talking

to Gaffer and Goodwife Pitkin. His was the only plow in the settlement, so its ownership gave him an undue sense of his own importance. He looked down his nose at Comfort as she came up.

"My father . . ." she began.

"He hath gone to the river with the other men," replied Goodman Rogers loudly, "to fetch the fish. Something delayeth them, mayhap they take their nooning by the river side."

"But he hath not his dinner . . ." began Comfort again.

"A goodly crop we shall have, God willing," said Goodwife Pitkin, "if we but do as the Indians taught us."

"Ay! The Indians be wise. Fish buried in the ground will rot and enrich the ground," added her husband.

"To enrich the ground be not enough!" Goodman Rogers frowned. "Even the seed-corn in the ground be not safe. The wolves will e'en come to dig up the corn-hills to get the buried fish. We must ask the Magistrate to set men to watch for fourteen nights, till the fish be well rotted."

"Ay!" agreed Gaffer Pitkin. " 'Tis a tiresome chore to stand all night in the cornfield, but needful to save the crop."

"So many calamities have we suffered from these evil beasts," said Goodwife Pitkin. "Never knew I such a hard winter, with so many wolves."

"We grow used to the creatures, they are become so bold!" laughed Goodman Rogers. "A sheep stolen from a pen or a dog torn to pieces or a wolf running down the path with a squealing pig in his jaws—'tis now a daily occurrence."

Comfort's face turned white.

"A wolf makes no more bones to run away with a pig than a dog to run away with a marrow bone!" added Gaffer Pitkin. "The bounty might be increased."

"My daughter Silence hath been sore affrighted . . ." began Goodwife Pitkin.

"Hath Silence, too, seen a wolf?" cried Comfort in distress.

"What is't, Comfort, lass? Why stare ye so? Have ye seen then a ghost?" asked Goodwife Pitkin.

But Comfort could not answer.

"Make haste, ye must not stand here idle, lass," the woman went on. "Take ye the dinner to thy father."

Comfort looked up into her face. "I'm afeared," she whispered.

"Nonsense! What fear ye then, in broad daylight?"

"A hungry wolf with great staring eyes . . ."

"Ye do but imagine things," said Goodwife Pitkin. "Go ye now, ere thy father be sore hungered."

Comfort grasped the kerchief bundles tightly. She crossed several fields and meadows. She walked cautiously, looking on all sides for the wolf. Then she came to the common pasture, which was tighty fenced in with high wooden palings.

Unlatching the gate, she entered, closing and latching it behind her. She felt safe inside the fence. The grass was growing lush and green now. It comforted her to know that the cows which had grown lean and poor with naught but coarse marsh grass hay to eat all winter would soon be fattening on the new grass and give rich milk again. With the she-goat dead, they would be in sore need of cow's milk for the babes. How would they ever manage?

She looked for Seaborn, but he was not to be seen. The field was large and partly over-grown with brush and young trees. She climbed to the top of a large rock, but still her brother was nowhere to be seen. She hoped that Tithingman Thatcher would not come and discover his absence. He would be fined for neglect of duty and doubtless lose his office as cow-keeper as well.

What could have taken Seaborn, always so conscientious, away from his duty? The wolf? Some other wild beast? An Indian? She shivered as she thought of the ever-present dangers besetting the little seaport town. But the cows grazed placidly. There was the fence, to keep them from harm. She breathed more easily.

Leaving Seaborn's dinner bundle beside the gate, she went without and latched it carefully behind her.

The river. She must go to the river, where the men were gathering fish. Each spring the ale-wives came up the river to spawn. When the waters receded each day at low tide, the fish lay exposed in the river bank. The men could get them easily.

She decided to go a roundabout way to avoid the forest. Wolves never came singly. They ran in packs. They came out of the forest to enter the town. A short-cut across a meadow brought her to the beach.

The tide was out. As usual on spring days, Indian children dug busily for clams and pelted with stones a few pigs who appeared. Indian squaws, fat and cumbersome, crawled about on the rocky shore just beyond the beach. Reaching and diving into the water, they pulled out huge green lobsters. Then they waddled to their huge basket hampers and threw them in.

Comfort sat down on the rocks. The presence of the friendly Indians made her forget her fears. Then she saw Know-God with the Indian boys.

She called out to him: "Why so many lobsters, Know-God?"

"Indians eat lobster," answered the boy. "Dry them for storage, too."

"How will they get them home?"

"Carry full baskets on their backs."

"Heavy?"

"Not as heavy as a dead deer."

Know-God seldom talked. But today he was friendly. Bare-backed and bare-legged as usual, he held in his hand a long staff, sharpened at the end with notches like saw-teeth. When he saw lobsters crawling in shallow water, he plunged the stick in the lobster's head and brought him up.

Other Indians boys were spearing fish. They threw in short wooden spears sharpened with fish-bone and attached to a sinew cord. With this cord, they drew in the fish after it was struck. Grunting and laughing, they pulled in fish after fish, then threw them into their baskets.

Comfort watched with interest. If only Seaborn were here. He liked all the Indian ways. Her mother said he was already more of an Indian than an English boy.

Know-God brought up a huge lobster with fierce claws. He held it aloft with a brave gesture. Comfort laughed.

What if Parson Humphrey could see him now? Although he was trying so valiantly to make him an English boy,

Know-God spent most of his time with the Indians. He hated white men's clothing and seldom wore it. He bore his frequent punishments with fortitude and continued to run away. He was happy with the Indians.

Suddenly Know-God gave a sharp cry and pointed.

On the rocks near the water's edge, Comfort saw a black bear staggering clumsily. He, too, was after lobsters. He thrust his great paw under the water and pulled one out.

"Our friend of the forest?" called Comfort.

"Mayhap!" answered Know-God.

But the bear did not enjoy his sport in peace for long. Quietly the Indian boys gathered together on the rocks, the women and children on the beach. At a signal from Know-God, the boys closed in on the bear. The beast dropped the lobster and clambered off the rocks to the sandy beach. Then all the Indians together gave chase.

All but Owl Woman, who came up to Comfort.

"We chase him home, let Indian braves kill him!" she explained. "Bear meat good, better than venison. Bear oil useful for many things."

Comfort and Owl Woman watched the bear as it dashed on all fours through the marshy meadow and off toward the forest, chased by the crowd of noisy Indians.

Then Comfort remembered her errand. She looked at the sun and knew it was past nooning.

"You go home now?" asked Owl Woman kindly.

"I go find my father," answered Comfort. "The men plant corn, get fish in the river."

"Get fish," repeated Owl Woman, with a smile of understanding. "Plant corn, good."

It was well past nooning when Comfort and the Indian squaw came to the river bank. But her father had had no time to think of food. There on the shore a dead animal lay outstretched.

Comfort turned to Owl Woman, thinking it must be the bear. The English men had killed the Indians' bear. The Indians would be angry, because they wanted it themselves. They liked bear meat better than venison and they wanted bear oil.

Then she looked again.

No, it was not the bear. It was a lean black wolf.

She clutched Owl Woman's hand. Then she fell a-sobbing as she leaned against the Indian squaw. The woman's arms pressed tightly round her shoulders.

"We planted a bait yestereven," cried Seaborn, coming forward to explain. "We imbedded a bunch of mackerel hooks in tallow, tying them first to a strong chain."

"A wolf had been visiting the river bed daily and stealing fish," said Old Goodman Jenney.

"Silence Pitkin hath been sore affrighted," put in Goodman Perkins. "The wolves be over-bold when they walk in the town in daylight and frighten the women-folk."

"When I drove the cows to pasture this morn," said Seaborn, "I saw a wolf with a goat in his mouth come galloping over the meadow. He came to the river, swallowed our hooks and they killed him. The chain held him fast, so he could not run off and die in the forest."

" 'Twas a fine she-goat he got . . ." said Goodman Jenney, pointing.

" 'Twas *our* she-goat, brother." Comfort raised her face and spoke.

"*Our* goat!" exclaimed Seaborn. "But I left her safe home in the pen."

Gaffer Partridge came up. "What say ye, lass?"

"Mother bade me tell thee . . ." began Comfort. But the tears came to her eyes and she could not speak.

Owl Woman patted her on the back and she began again: "I sat on the milking-stool a-milking, when over the fence leaped a wolf. His eyes were red, they burned like fire . . ."

"There, there, my lambie!" cried Gaffer Partridge tenderly. "Be ye no longer affrighted. Thy wolf lies dead there, on the river bank. He will never steal goats again."

The men, hearing Comfort's story, felt strong sympathy with the Partridge family both for the fright and the loss of their she-goat.

"The head and hide be thine, Gaffer Partridge," they said.

Sending young Web Perkins to the common pasture to keep watch on the cows, they ordered Seaborn to go to the village with the head of the animal, to hang it on the meeting house door and claim the bounty.

Owl Woman spoke up: "Forty beaver skins for the hide," she begged.

"Ay!" cried Gaffer Partridge. "'Tis thine! See ye that Black Cloud bringeth them in, when next he comes to the village."

"He too lazy!" grunted the squaw. "Owl Woman bring them herself." She held out Aunt Charity's silver spoon, which she wore round her neck. Gaffer Partridge knew he could trust her.

Comfort watched Owl Woman drag the wolf's body off toward the forest. When the men returned to the cornfield with their baskets of fish, she walked beside them.

"Go ye home now, lass," said Gaffer Partridge. "Fret not, thy wolf is dead."

When she reached home, they all crowded round to hear her story.

"Thy wolf!" cried Waitstill. "Its head hangeth even now from the meeting house door."

Comfort turned to Aunt Charity. "Must I then go look at it?"

"Nay, child! Ye can dodge round the corner!"

CHAPTER TWELVE

A Pound
of Sorrow

*E*arly one morning in midsummer, Seaborn Partridge, gun over shoulder, followed the cows to pasture. He blew his horn lustily as he passed the Lumpkin house, then waited. The Lumpkin cow did not appear.

He heard loud shouts within the house. Then the door burst open and Patty Tucker, disheveled and untidy, came flying out. Immediately she slowed down her pace and walked to the barn.

Next, out from the door came Gaffer Lumpkin, falling headlong. He lay in the pathway and groaned. He raised himself, felt of the great lump on his head and groaned again.

"Sluggard! Snail! Lazy lout!" shouted his wife. "Get ye gone!"

Gaffer Lumpkin rose to his feet and walked away.

"Drat the woman!" he said in a low voice, as he passed the cow-keeper. "She hitted me on the head with her broomstaff."

Goody Lumpkin herself came out of the house with a basket on her arm and marched off toward town. Finally the barn door opened, the cow came out, and then Patty. She glanced in at the house door, to make sure of her mistress' absence, then spoke to Seaborn.

"How fares thy sweet aunt, Mistress Charity?"

"Why ask ye?" growled Seaborn. "Look, the sun riseth. Ye have made me late."

"If I could but see her . . ." began Patty.

Seaborn frowned. "What business have ye then with my aunt?"

"Naught that I can tell thee!" cried Patty gaily. She swished her skirts, reached into a pocket and brought out her pipe. From another pocket she brought tobacco and began to fill the bowl.

Seaborn stared.

"A pipe?" he cried. "Smokest thou? From whence then have ye pipe and tobacco?"

"From the Indians who grow it," answered Patty sullenly. Then she changed her tone. "If ye be so cross, I shan't tell thee the news."

"What news?" asked Seaborn, suspicious.

"I rose before the dawn," said Patty mysteriously. "I looked out my window and what did I see but a row of Indian braves going past . . . on tip-toe . . . so quiet they were, not a sound they made . . ."

"What Indians were they?" demanded Seaborn.

"How then should I know?" laughed Patty. "Me but just come over from the streets of Old London Town—all Indians look alike to me! But . . . one was young and handsome, 'twas he gave me tobacco!"

"But ye were in bed! Ye but looked out the window!" said Seaborn, doubting her tale.

"I threw on my gown first and ran out," answered Patty glibly.

"Young and handsome?" asked Seaborn. "Had he a scar from ear to mouth?"

"Ay!" said Patty agreeably. "He told me his name . . ."

"Was it Josias?"

"Why, how then did *ye* know?" cried Patty, laughing.

"The son of the great Sachem Chickatawbut! But he hath bad blood, he consorteth with . . ." Seaborn turned on the servant maid furious with anger. "Have ye reported? Have ye warned the Captain and the Watch?"

"Oh, no," said Patty. "I never thought o' that."

"Never thought of it?" shouted Seaborn. "Never thought of the safety of the settlement? Ye be more corrupt than they say ye be!"

Hastily and with a scared look on her face, Patty thrust her pipe with its unsmoked tobacco back into her pocket. "Ye won't tittle-tattle, will ye?"

Seaborn did not hear. He was already on his way back to town.

Patty glanced wildly around. She saw the town cows wandering along the roadside and in the meadow.

"The cows! The cows!" she yelled. But Seaborn did not hear.

"I be not cow-keeper!" she added to herself. " 'Tis no concern o' mine." Shrugging her shoulders, she went back into the house, found some breakfast and ate it.

At intervals through the morning, half-hearted snatches of song burst through the open door and windows. But it was not until well after nooning that Patty came outdoors again, puffing on her pipe. She walked to the back of the house, and there where the brickwork of the oven protruded in a great hump, climbed leisurely up. Raised to an elevation of some four feet above the ground, she looked over the Lumpkins' cornfield. The half-grown corn rippled and waved in the breeze. Patty stared, for she thought she saw something moving.

"Drat them hawgs!" she cried. "They got me one beating—I don't want another."

Turning to the roof's eave, she knocked the half-burned tobacco out of her pipe. Then she jumped down, picked up a stick and entered the cornfield.

She hadn't gone far when an unusual sight met her eyes, but it was not the pigs which she had expected to see. It was cows. Several cows were lying on top of the green cornstalks. A great patch of half-grown corn was trampled under foot.

"Laws-a-mercy me!" cried Patty, in sudden distress. Then more brightly: "The town cows! Won't the cow-keeper ketch it!"

With her stick she began to belabor the cows, but they did not rise to their feet. She poked hard at one over-fat cow, but it did not move.

"Lay there then, and see if I care!" she exclaimed.

She started back to the house. At the edge of the cornfield she stopped in her tracks and stared.

"Laws . . . a . . . mer . . . cy . . . me! Oh, good Lord, what 'ave I done?" she sobbed.

The roof of the Lumpkin house was in flames.

Patty did not need to be told how it had happened. She reached in her pocket and pulled out her pipe. She looked at it with loathing and disgust, as if it were to blame for her own carelessness. Angrily she threw it down and ground it with her heel until it was buried in dirt.

"I did but shake out . . . my pipe . . . by the thatch!" she cried in a weak voice.

Then she ran as fast as she could go, screaming. After a time her screams died down and she ran a-whimpering.

Goodman Pettijohn, the cooper, who lived in the nearest house, came flying. Bravely he filled a piggin with water and entered the house to put out the fire. He poured water on the fireplace in the first room, then in the second. Not till the piggin was empty did he notice that both fires were already out before he came. Only a few burnt-out brands lay on the cold hearths.

Then he looked up. Through the cracks in the floor boards overhead, he saw the attic chamber filled with smoke, and at one side, bright flames lighting the whole interior.

"Good Lord, have mercy! Good Lord, deliver us!" He fell on his knees. Seeing Patty gaping open-mouthed beside him, he yanked her down, crying: "Pray, lass, pray!" Patty fell on her knees beside him. "Send us not to Hell before our time, good Lord . . ."

Patty Tucker never prayed so hard in her life before. But the prayers did not stop the flames. The dry straw-thatched roof was like tinder and soon the whole house was ablaze.

From all sides the neighbors came flying—the Pitkins, the Rogers, the Eliots and many others. They found the old man and the servant maid on their knees oblivious to danger, and pulled them out to safety. They lugged chairs and chests and trenchers and iron pots to the yard outside. Then they stood helplessly by and watched the flames mount higher and higher.

Suddenly a loud scream rent the air, and the wild figure of a girl dashed in through the smoke-filled door. The people gasped and stared. Desperate minutes passed while no one moved. Then out through flames and smoke came the same figure, singed and soot-covered now, staggering uncertainly. The girl pressed a silver porringer to her lips and kissed it again and again. Then, sobbing, she fell to the ground, exhausted.

. . . .

Goody Lumpkin meanwhile paid a morning call on her close friend and bosom companion, Goodwife Minching. From her basket she emptied a mess of fresh young garden peas; then accepted a gift of two cakes of dried yellow saffron.

"So useful for coloring and flavoring dishes for the table," said Goodwife Minching.

"So precious, too," answered Goody Lumpkin. "Thy saffron crocus plants from Essex be almost the only ones in the settlement."

The women walked to the gate and put their heads together.

"Heard ye that the Widow Cummings hath been hailed up in Court at last?" whispered Goodwife Minching.

"A vain, giddy young hussy! 'Twill but serve her right!" exclaimed Goody Lumpkin. "Her fair face and extravagant apparel do already condemn her. Remember ye not how the Magistrate himself did reprimand her when first she came, for immoderate taste in that London mulberry gown of hers?"

"I felt it my duty to admonish her once," said Goodwife Minching, "but she hardened her heart and refused to listen."

A boy ran up the path. Then several men from the brick works went hurrying by.

"Such unseemly haste!" cried Goody Lumpkin, staring. "The tithing-men be lazy and neglect their duty this day."

Freedom Rogers and Hate-Evil Eliot ran past. "Look ye! Look ye!" they cried, pointing.

Goody Lumpkin looked and saw more people running, and in the sky above, a black cloud. She and Goodwife Minching began to run too.

But heavy footsteps came behind them and a man's heavy hand grasped them by their shoulders. "Stop, I order ye, gossips!"

The women halted their steps.

"Go ye now, soberly walking," cried Timothy Thatcher, the Tithing-man.

The women took a few steps, then began to hurry.

"First I seed ye standing idle at the gatepost gossiping," he went on, "practicing tale-bearing from house to house, setting differences between neighbors. Now I've ketched ye *running!*"

The women scarcely heard him. Seeing many people, all running in the same direction, and hearing loud, excited cries, they broke into a run.

"Stop, I order ye, gossips!" shouted Thatcher. "I forbid such unseemly haste."

But the women only ran faster. The nearer they came to the Lumpkin home, the faster they ran. Timothy Thatcher forgot sober walking himself, and ran, trying to catch up. Goodwife Minching got there first. Then came Goody Lumpkin, panting.

"My pewter platter!" she screamed, as soon as she caught her breath. "My seven spoons, my warming pan, my porringers . . . my brass pot, my iron pot, my griddle . . . my noggins and my trenchers . . . my chairs and my table . . . my straw tick and pillows . . . my stuff petticoat and waistcoat . . ."

"Gaffer Lumpkin then had naught?" broke in Goodwife Pitkin.

"He had a coat with silver buttons—it be burnt, too!" wailed Goody Lumpkin, wringing her hands.

Then her eye fell on Patty Tucker, sitting melancholy and distressed, on an overturned tub.

"This be *thy* mischief, wench!" cried her mistress, rushing over and pulling her to her feet. "Ye worthless blockhead, ye careless fool, ye neglectful sluggard, ye . . ."

"Hold thy tongue, wife!" cried Gaffer Lumpkin, now arrived on the scene. "Want ye the whole settlement to hear?"

But Goody Lumpkin, once started, was hard to stop.

"Ay!" she shouted. "I want the whole settlement to hear. This evil-minded servant maid of mine hath wilfully burnt down my house. Sit ye by and say naught?"

"How know ye then she did it?" inquired Goodwife Rogers.

"Ain't she the only person left in the house the whole day? Ain't she threatened a hundred times to pay me back? Who else could 'ave done it?"

Stuffing her silver porringer into her pocket, Patty burst out in loud sobs. The very sound of her grief seemed to proclaim her guilt. The people looked at the girl, then at the angry, wind-driven flames, and they were forced to agree with the woman. They turned cold shoulders on Patty.

"As for you, husband," cried Goody Lumpkin loudly, "why was ye not here to keep the wilful wench from such mischief? What mean ye, going gadding at mid-day? What mean ye?"

"I did come but now from the hay-field," said Gaffer Lumpkin slowly, "whither ye sent me before sun-rising this morn."

But even this did not stop her. The scolding woman, her tongue now well loosened, shouted and argued, accused and complained. All her neighbors came in for strenuous tongue-lashings. So busy scolding was she that she failed to notice the approach of a man in armor, with a long staff in hand, the Constable himself. She did not see him step behind a tree where he could hear without being seen. She did not see the smile which played round his stern lips.

Nor did she see a cow stagger out from her cornfield. Not until the assembled people turned away from her and stared at the animal did her eyes glance in that direction.

"My cow!" she screamed. "What ails it?"

She turned on Patty. "Oped ye not the shed door this morn?"

"I oped it, Ma'am! I oped it!" cried Patty, in wild protest.

"Went not the cow out to pasture with the cow-keeper?" demanded Goody Lumpkin.

Patty hung her head. "I know not," she said in a low voice. "I did but busy myself with housewifery . . ."

Several men came hurrying in from the cornfield, whither they had gone to investigate.

"Three cows be dead!" they announced. "They be bloated, they be foundered on green corn. They have et green corn since early dawn."

The woman cried out in distress: "Oh, law me!" "Oh, laws-a-mercy-me!"

The Lumpkin cow lay down in the shade of the tree near where the Constable stood, and died before their eyes.

Goody Lumpkin stared, speechless. She could find no scolding words to say. She clapt her apron over her head and fell to weeping loudly. Many other women wept. Four dead cows were a great loss to the settlement.

"Where then be the cow-keeper?" cried the men.

Constable Cartwright stepped out from behind the tree.

"Tithing-man Thatcher," he cried, "cometh not the cow-keeper from one of thy families?"

Tithing-man Thatcher cleared his throat. "Ay, good sir. Seaborn Partridge be cow-keeper . . . a righteous lad . . ."

"What then hath happened to young Partridge?" continued the Constable.

"Oh, good sir," cried Patty, brushing her tears away and stepping forward. "He went early this morn to tell the news to the Captain and the Watch."

"The news? What news?" asked the Constable.

"Indians, good sir!" cried Patty mysteriously. "The enemy!"

"Hush, lass!" The Constable bent over her hurriedly. "Say it not aloud. Whisper thy news in my ear."

Patty cupped her hands and whispered. As her story lengthened, the man's eyes opened wide. He stood staring and thoughtful for a moment, then recovered himself. The people, standing silent, waited.

"This be indeed a day of sorrow for the settlement," boomed Constable Cartwright in his heavy voice. "Serious matters demand our immediate attention, so the calamity before us must wait. It will, however, be taken up at the next meeting of the town Court. At that time, the following persons will appear to answer charges brought this day against them:

"Patty Tucker, redemptioner, for wilfully setting fire to the house of her mistress.

"Goody Lumpkin, for being a notorious scold.

"Seaborn Partridge, cow-keeper, for neglect of duty."

A murmur of awe, surprise and sorrow rose from the crowd.

"Disperse yourselves!" cried the Constable. "Stand ye not here all the day idle! Get ye gone to your homes!"

"But I got no home to go to!" wailed Goody Lumpkin.

"Nor I!" echoed her husband in a faint voice.

The Constable looked at the pair. "An English wigwam by the seacoast stands empty!" he snorted.

Goody Lumpkin picked up some pots, her spoons and a pile of clothing, and started off. Gaffer Lumpkin gathered up as many things as he could and trotted behind her.

Patty Tucker looked after them longingly. After all, a home was a home no matter how poor the place nor how badly one was treated there. She gathered up a few broken trenchers and hurried to catch up.

But her mistress turned on her angrily. "Wretch!" she cried. "Get ye gone from my sight! Back to England ye kin go, for aught I care. Let me never see thy face again!"

"But, wife, I paid for five years' service," whined Gaffer Lumpkin, "and I promised the lass a she-goat to start out in life."

The man's words sounded almost kind and brought new hope to the girl. But Goody Lumpkin's heart was hard like stone.

"Get ye gone from my sight, wretch!" she shouted. "Never shall ye cross my threshold or eat my bread again!"

" 'Tis sour anyhow!" muttered Patty under her breath. "And I putted a toad in thy kettle of milk!"

The neighbors had all gone away when Patty returned. Beside the smoking ashes she sat down on the overturned tub. She cried as she had never cried before. She cried as if her heart would break with sorrow.

CHAPTER THIRTEEN

Do Unto Others

The curfew bell rang and the town was still—
all but the chirpings and chatterings of birds and
insects, the rustle of leaves and the sighing of
the wind. These, by man's order, could not be stilled.

"Nine o' the clock and a fair breeze blowing!" came the
cry of the night Watchman.

Suddenly a loud knock shook the batten door of the
Partridge house. Cries and shrieks rang out.

"Let me go, I tell ye! Loose my arm!" a shrill voice
screamed. "I know where I be a-goin', ye need not drag
me and pull me and pommel me and push me . . ." A
great scuffling rattled and shook the heavy door.

When Gaffer Partridge opened it, Patty Tucker fell in
a heap at his feet and rolled over on the floor.

"This wench . . ." stammered the Watch, breathless, "insisted on coming here . . . I tried to make her tell me her business, but she bit and scratched me sore."

He held his lantern high and its feeble rays fell on the heap of rags which covered the shaking, quivering girl.

"It be my duty to examine all night-walkers after nine o' the clock at night," the man went on, "but this wench refuses to explain her light conduct, her gadding about at night."

"I told ye to pay no heed to me, to go off and be on thy way and mind thine own affairs! I told thee I knew

what I was a-doin' and 'twas no business o' thine! I telled thee to let me alone!" A wild storm of protest broke from Patty.

"Cease thy foolish chatter, wench," cried the Watch, "or I'll hand ye over to the Constable yet." He turned to Gaffer Partridge. "Had I not known ye for an honorable man, good sir, who countenances not wrong-doing or evil practices, I would not have brought her here . . ."

"Ye brought me not, ye old fool!" screamed Patty. "I came myself. Ye did but try to hamper me and yank me in t'other direction, but I bit ye good and kicked ye and hurted ye in a dozen places and ye know it. Thanks be to God's mercy, I got here at last." Her outburst over, the girl fell a-sobbing.

Meanwhile Goodwife Partridge, Aunt Charity and the children had been aroused and stood silently watching.

"Ye wish to have the maid here, good sir?" asked the Watch. "Or, shall I take her in custody until the morn cometh? This is a wanton offense. She can be hauled up before the Magistrate for being abroad at night and for disturbing the peace."

Gaffer Partridge looked down at the girl and pondered thoughtfully. Aunt Charity touched him gently on the arm. He turned to the Watch and said: "Let her stay here, sir. Thank ye for bringing her."

"Good even, good sir."

The heavy door closed with a thud. The Watchman's retreating footsteps rang out in the quiet night. Then came his cry, gradually sounding fainter: "Past nine o' the clock and a fair breeze blowing! Past nine o' the clock . . ."

The departure of the Watch's lantern left the room in darkness. Gaffer Partridge felt his way to the fireplace, stirred the coals and lit a splinter of candlewood. This he stuck into a chink between the stones of the fireplace. It threw a feeble ray of light across the room.

It was Goodwife Partridge who spoke first. "She hath made this grievous trouble for Seaborn. She hath wilfully burnt down her mistress' house. We want her not here."

"I did but tell the cow-keeper that I seed Indians go a-marching by the house, Ma'am," whimpered Patty. "If he said they was bad Indians and if he went a-running to tell the Captain, how could I help it, Ma'am? And if he left the town cows to wander in the cornfield, how could I help it, Ma'am? I called him long and loud to come back, but he came not. And I never *did* set the house on fire a-purpose, Ma'am. I never *did* want the house to burn up, so I'd not have no home to go to, and not even a pallet bed to sleep on, Ma'am!" She sobbed again.

"Hath Patty been a sinful girl, Mother?" Waitstill's clear voice rang out in the quietness.

"Hush, hush!" cried Goodwife Partridge. She looked at the children standing in the door. "Get ye back to bed, childer! Make haste!"

The children scrambled out of sight.

"She has no place to go," said Aunt Charity in a low voice.

"We can't turn her out in the night," said Gaffer Partridge.

"Let her go to the gaol where she rightly belongs," said Goodwife Partridge harshly. "She hath brought disgrace on us all. Let her suffer for her sins. A pallet bed in the gaol awaits her."

"No, no, no, no!" cried Patty.

" 'Tis past nine o' the clock," said Gaffer Partridge slowly. "She will make a loud outcry and disturb the peace."

Silence fell again as the candlewood flickered. Then the flame went out, leaving the room in darkness.

"I will take her to sleep in my bed," said Charity. "Come, Patty."

Goodwife Partridge did not reply.

The girl rose to her feet, took Mistress Charity's hand, and climbed the narrow stairs behind her.

The next morning Patty Tucker stayed in the attic chamber. Mistress Charity brought food for her to eat. She brought warm water for her bath. She washed her clothes and dried them. She scrubbed the girl's hair and head. She cut off the singed ends of her hair. A subdued and quiet Patty as well as a clean one replaced the wild and distraught girl of the night before.

"What say they of me downstairs?" asked Patty.

"They have not so much as spoken thy name," replied Mistress Charity.

"Why not, Ma'am?" asked Patty.

"They strive to be cheerful as is their duty. Thy name bringeth sadness."

"Will Goodwife Partridge send me to gaol?"

"Not till I give my consent," replied Mistress Charity.

"Be Gaffer Partridge angry?"

"Ay! He and his wife be sore vexed with thee, for ye have brought grievous trouble on their son."

"Will they then beat me?"

"No, Patty."

"But Goody Lumpkin did always beat me when she was angry."

"Ye be at the Lumpkin house no longer."

"Oh, Ma'am, I do so love it here, let me but stay and live with thee and I will serve thee right willingly. I will work my fingers to the bone for thee, I will never again be wicked or disobedient."

Mistress Charity studied the girl thoughtfully. "Tell me, Patty," she began, "did ye ever try in truth to please thy mistress?"

"Nay, not oft!" said Patty. "She did naught but find fault. She's but a fault-finder and a scold. 'Twas useless to try to please her."

"Did ye ever think ye might please God, even if 'twas impossible to please Goody Lumpkin?"

Patty hung her head in shame. "I never thought o' that." Then she looked up fearfully. "Will He then punish me for being so wicked and rebellious and evil . . ." Patty fell a-sobbing. "I hated her so for all her unkind words and deeds."

"Did ye strive to return kind words and deeds? It hurteth not the tongue to speak fair words."

"Nay, I never thought o' that." Patty sobbed afresh.

"Know ye not the Scripture saith: 'Do unto others as ye would that they should do unto thee?' Think on these words, Patty."

"Will Goody Lumpkin send me back to Old England, Ma'am?"

"I know not, Patty." Mistress Charity's face was sober. "Don't let her, don't let her!" cried Patty. "If I could live with thee, Ma'am, 'twould be easy to be good. I would never be wilful or disobedient or . . ."

"How can I believe you, Patty?" asked Mistress Charity. "Ye have made me fair promises before, but have not kept them. Ye have indeed been a wicked, sinful girl and I be sore displeased. Ye have let Satan so rule thy heart, ye have crowded God out. How think ye to get people to love thee, if ye be always wicked and evil and never kind and loving?"

"Must I then be kind and loving, so people will love *me?*" She smiled faintly. "I never thought o' that."

" 'Tis time ye began to think, then, Patty," replied Mistress Charity. "You get, in this world, even what you give." Taking up her psalm book, she read a psalm aloud:

> *"He gently-leads me, quiet-waters by*
> *He doth retain my soul for His name's sake*
> *In paths of justice leads-me-quietly.*
> *Yea, though I walk in dale of deadly-shade*
> *I'll fear no ill, for with me Thou wilt be*
> *Thy rod, Thy staff, they shall comfort me."*

Telling Patty to repeat the psalm to herself, she went away and left the girl alone.

Days passed and the Partridge family grew accustomed to Patty's presence. She made herself generally useful. She helped with the cooking, the cleaning, the washing. She kept God-be-thanked out of mischief. She weeded in the vegetable patch, she worked in the cornfield. She milked the cow which had recently been allotted to the care of the Partridges. She was a subdued and quiety Patty, quick, neat and handy, willing and anxious to please. When her tasks were done, she sat down and knitted on stockings for the younger children, allowing herself no idle moments.

Goodwife Partridge, angry at first, was soon won over by the girl's industry and cheerfulness. She saw too the strong hold that Charity had over the girl and recognized that her sister's kindness might be more effective than Goody Lumpkin's brutality and scolding. She remembered her sister's wish, upon her first arrival, that she had taken the girl for a servant. What months of suffering the lass might have been spared, had she never fallen into Goody Lumpkin's hands! But perhaps this was God's way . . . maybe Charity could do more with her now than she could have done then.

Goodwife Partridge said no more about gaol, and Patty stayed on.

Thankful and Comfort found her a helpful and gay companion. They enjoyed her help with their daily duties, her lively chatter and her gay and tuneful songs. God-be-thanked came to love her and Waitstill followed her about like a devoted puppy, calling her "Our Patty."

Only Seaborn avoided her and never spoke. At meal times, he ate hastily, keeping his eyes on his food. When the meal was over, he rushed away from the house.

But one time Seaborn and Patty met. Patty brought her piggin to the cow-shed and waited there till Seaborn returned from the pasture with the cow.

"I be right sorry for the trouble I bringed on thee," said Patty.

Seaborn turned away. Patty followed and timidly touched his sleeve.

"Ye lied to me!" cried Seaborn angrily.

"Nay, 'twas no lie," said Patty. "I *did* see Indians close by the house and Josias, the young brave, said 'twas an enemy tribe come to search out . . ."

"Captain Stoddard disbelieved when I told him," replied Seaborn bitterly. "All the Watch laughed at me. They said we have naught to fear from such weak and friendly Indians as the Massachusetts. Only Know-God, who is friend to all Indians, believed, but the Captain laughed at him too. Ye lied! Ye delighted to have me neglect my duty, to have the cows die, to have me disgraced!"

"I telled thee the truth!" protested Patty.

"Ye lied! A wicked liar ye be!"

Seaborn stalked angrily away.

. . . .

Several days later, at Master Gershom Flagg's shop on the green, the Widow Cummings made a leisurely selection of dress-goods and trimmings. Rolls of fustian, shag, duffle and kersey lay before her. Master Flagg hovered near, showing his customer every attention.

"What color prefer ye?"

Widow Cummings questioned the young girl beside her.

"I like all colors so they be red!" cried Patty, clapping her hands together.

Red shag and red kersey for two new gowns were measured off. Then rolls of calico, dowlas and holland were brought out. From these also, the girl made her own selection for neck-cloths, coifs and falling collars. Her eyes sparkled with pleasure, though her demeanor was quiet and subdued.

The shop bell tinkled. A woman opened the door and shouted: "I cannot pay thee at once, good sir, but have ye then fustian, good sir, to cast upon the bed for a sheet . . . ?"

The words faded away and the woman stared. "So ye ain't slept in yon ashes, after all!" She fixed her eyes on Patty Tucker.

It was Goody Lumpkin.

"No, Ma'am, I ain't!" snapped Patty. "And I ain't slep' in no hole in the ground, or in no dirty, filthy English wigwam, I ain't. I be serving maid to a gentlewoman, I be. I bide in a fair house with boards on the floor and glass in the windows. I don't wear cast-off rags no more, since I have chose for myself two new gowns of enduring cloth, bright red, not sad-colored; neck-cloths of flowered calico, falling collars of fine holland and aprons with colorful stripes!"

"Patty!" cried Widow Cummings reproachfully.

"Buy ye then fustian sheets, Ma'am," continued Patty, now thoroughly aroused, "to cast upon thy pallet bed on the dirt floor of thy miserable hut? And think ye Master Flagg will give thee sheets ye cannot pay for?"

"Patty!" cried Widow Cummings again. "Patty, please. Ye will but regret these hasty words."

"Ay!" broke in Goody Lumpkin, her eyes flashing. "When ye lie on thy pallet bed in yon gaol, Patty Tucker, when ye lie in the dirty, stinking hold of the boat that takes thee back to Old England, then will ye regret your wicked, sinful ways, how ye did sore vex thy honest, well-meaning mistress and make thy loving master's days a torment. Ye will regret how ye did wilfully set thy mistress' house afire and burn it to the ground! Ye will have plenty of regrets to plague and pester thee, but small good will it do thee then!"

Widow Cummings hastily paid for her purchases and left the shop, pulling Patty, laden down with parcels, behind her. The scolding woman's angry words were carried to them on the breeze and rang in their ears long

after they were out of hearing.

"I be sore displeased with thee, Patty," said Mistress Charity, as soon as they reached the attic chamber. "Remember ye not what I said about returning good for evil?"

"I did but tell her the truth!" muttered Patty sullenly.

"It ill becomes thee to boast, Patty Tucker," said Mistress Charity severely. "I did but buy thee new garments to cover thy nakedness, since ye had but one gown torn to rags. I bought them not to encourage vain boasting. To wear fine clothes above one's station in life is a sin and brings sure punishment. I did but let thee share my bed, since ye had no bed but the dry ashes of thy carelessness to sleep in. I took thee into my sister's house despite her wishes.

"This is no light matter, Patty Tucker. Ye are here for a short time only. At the next meeting of the town Court, ye must appear and answer to the most serious charge of wilfully setting fire to thy mistress' house and burning it to the ground with all its contents. This crime, in Old England and New, is punishable by death. The lightest sentence ye can expect, if thy guilt be proven, is banishment from the Colony. Goody Lumpkin loves thee not and will say hard things against thee. She will never rest till she hath had her revenge. Her prophecy may be right. If they spare thee for thy youth, they will send thee back to England."

"Oh, no, Ma'am, no!" cried Patty in distress. "Don't let them! Keep me here with thee! Don't let them!"

"This time, Patty," said Mistress Charity, "no word of mine can help thee."

CHAPTER FOURTEEN

Day of Rest

A salt breeze blew soft, yet vigorous and refreshing, from off the sea on a Sabbath morn in late summer. Peace hung over the huddled houses of the village and the seldom-used fort on the hill.

At nine of the clock, the sharp clamor of a drum broke out. Preserved Rogers, drummer boy, marched from Parson Humphrey's to Gaffer Partridge's house and back again, beating vigorously. The four tithing-men scurried through the village, each searching out the homes of the families under his charge, and commanding all except the bed-ridden to go to meeting.

Timothy Thatcher burst open the door of the Partridge house. He found all the members arrayed in their best garments, waiting. Quickly they stepped into line. Gaffer Partridge bore his gun on his shoulder, being one of the Guard for the day. Beside him walked his wife, carrying God-be-thanked. Then came the two girls, Thankful and Comfort, with Waitstill between them. Behind followed Widow Cummings and Patty Tucker, redemptioner.

Timothy Thatcher counted noses. "Eight! Ay, that be right!" he murmured. "Ye cow-keeper be allowed two Sabbaths out of three for worship that his morals be not neglected." He looked over the group again. "But where be the cow-keeper? Be it not his turn for meeting?"

"Seaborn tendeth pasture this day," answered Gaffer Partridge.

Thatcher scratched his head. "How then number ye eight?" Then his eye fell on Patty Tucker. He coughed and sputtered. "Who be she?"

"Patty Tucker, if it please ye, good sir," said Patty, with a curtsey.

"The wench who burnt the house down?" cried the Tithing-man. "What be she a-doin' here? She belongeth to the Lumpkins in the English wigwam, and the wigwams belong to Tithing-man Peabody. 'Tis Peabody's task to look after her. I'll have naught to do with her, I won't."

"Good sir," said Widow Cummings sweetly, "if I be responsible for the lass's conduct, will ye not kindly permit her to sit by my side?"

"Why . . . er . . ." answered Thatcher, "the Magistrate hath not instructed us, but . . . well, I reckon she can."

The little procession moved on, joined soon by the Pitkins, Sewards and others. All walked in silence with sober faces, not daring to speak or smile or laugh. Passing the stocks, pillory and whipping-post on the village green, they arrived at the thatch-roofed meeting house. Through the door, blood-stained from the heads of many wolves, without a glance at the armed guard standing at attention, they entered solemnly. The men took their places on narrow benches on the minister's right, the women, girls and younger children on his left. The boys made their way to the pulpit and sat down on the steps.

In front of the pulpit sat the elders, in front of them the deacons, and in the foremost bench Magistrate, Captain and Constable. The men of the Guard, led by a sergeant, sat in a body on the men's side, each putting his musket or fire-lock down near him.

As Parson Humphrey entered, clad in long black Genevan robe and close-fitting black cap, the congregation rose in token of respect and remained standing until after he had entered the pulpit and was seated. The absence of his adopted son was plainly noticed. It was rumored that Know-God had run away to the Indians again, and this time meant never to return.

The first prayer was but begun when a hubbub arose. Tithing-man Peabody entered, hauling two young boys in by their collars. The congregation looked, expecting to see the runaway Indian boy brought back, but they were disappointed. The culprits were Freedom Rogers and Hate-Evil Eliot.

"Sabbath-breaking!" announced Peabody. "Sitting on a fence at ten o' the clock on a Sabbath morn!"

"We did but look out for enemy Indians!" piped young Freedom defiantly.

"Play not on the Lord's Day, for the Devil will be thy playfellow!" said Tithing-man Peabody, rapping the boy's head with the brass knob on the end of his rod.

After the expounding of a chapter of the Bible, a psalm was sung by the congregation line by line, as Deacon Hollingworth read it out:

"Have mercy Lord on me I pray
for man would me devour,
He fighteth with me day by day
and troubleth me each hour.

Mine enemies daily enterprise
to swallow me outright
To fight against me many rise,
O thou most high of might."

Then Parson Humphrey rose in the pulpit and began his sermon. The breeze from the sea died down and the late summer sun shone hot. It glared in at the closed windows, where flies and wasps buzzed against the panes. The room was close and airless.

The boys on the pulpit steps grew restless, and their feet began to scuffle back and forth. Little children nodded, then fell asleep on their mothers' laps. Old Goodman Jenney began to snore comfortably, when Tithing-man Thatcher stepped up. With the foxtail end of his rod, he tickled his upturned nose and woke the man with a start.

Patty Tucker listened idly to Parson Humphrey's thirteenthly and fourteenthly. She watched Tithing-man Peabody step up and turn the hour-glass at the minister's side, as his monotonous voice droned on. Then her attention wandered and she glanced out the window. She saw a figure moving in the distance. Wondering who could be abroad at this hour, she stared more intently.

A woman with loose black hair streaming out behind

her, came running down the winding path. Patty nudged Widow Cummings. She too looked out.

Tithing-man Thatcher saw the nudge. He lifted his rod, then dropped it to the floor with a noisy clatter. "Look ye!" he cried out.

"Owl Woman, Black Cloud's squaw, cometh!" announced Widow Cummings. Her clear voice rang out above the Parson's droning tones. The people sat up briskly.

The squaw came to a window and peered in. She lifted the silver spoon which she wore round her neck and beckoned frantically to Widow Cummings, who rose to her feet.

"But . . . this be out of order . . ." cried Tithing-man Thatcher, helplessly.

"Send one of the men!" ordered Constable Cartwright from the front seat.

"Send one of the Guard with his weapon!" shouted the Magistrate.

"If Know-God were but here!" cried Parson Humphrey.

"Good sirs," said Widow Cummings calmly, "Owl Woman wishes to have speech with me. Pray be not alarmed. There is no cause for anxiety."

Timothy Thatcher scratched his head. " 'Tis a ticklish point," he said, "we have not been instructed . . ."

Hastily Widow Cummings left the building, where fear now, instead of contentment and peace, reigned.

Thatcher and the other tithing-men stared out the windows. The men of the Guard grasped their guns and stood ready. Parson Humphrey, with a worried and anxious expression, continued his sermon. But no one listened.

Widow Cummings returned, but she said not a word. She smiled at the assembly and sat down in her place.

During the prayer which followed the sermon, the door flew open without warning, and two boys dashed in. The first was Seaborn Partridge, cow-keeper. The people gasped, for the second was Know-God Humphrey, the runaway Indian boy, come back of his own accord.

"What meaneth this?" shouted Seaborn loudly. "The guard by the meeting house door fast asleep! I be come to tell ye the settlement is in sore danger!"

"Lord, save us!" "Good Lord, protect us!" cried the people, leaving their seats and crowding close.

"Please to explain, lad!" ordered the Magistrate.

Know-God stood aside to let Seaborn talk.

"The sun was but three hours high," said he, "when I noticed a cow was missing. I hunted through the woods and brush of the pasture and came on a place where the palings of the fence were broken down. When I went out to search for the cow, I saw a group of Indian warriors emerge from the forest. They climbed up on a large boulder, they did point to the fort on the hill, to the ships in the harbor, to the . . ."

"Be they Massachusetts? Ye know the Massachusetts'

headgear?" The sharp question came from Captain Stoddard.

"Josias, son of Chickatawbut, and his braves were there," Seaborn replied. "The others were Tarratines."

"Tarratines!" cried the people, filled with sudden fear.

"How knew ye they were Tarratines?" demanded the Captain.

"Know-God was with them," said Seaborn. "He slipped away and came and told me."

"Know-God!" gasped the people. "Know-God consorting with Tarratines!"

"These same braves made an early morning visit to the settlement some weeks ago," Seaborn went on. "I gave thee due warning, but ye believed me not. Only Know-God believed me. Josias knoweth the fort hath no guns ready, no armed men on guard . . ."

"Know-God is traitor! Know-God hath told Josias!" cried Goodman Rogers and others.

"Nay, say not so!" cried Seaborn. "Know-God came to warn us of our danger. Tell them, Know-God, what ye heard."

"The Tarratines make ready to attack!" answered the Indian boy.

Captain Stoddard turned to the congregation. "The Tarratines be less savage and cruel than the Mohawks, but next deadly as enemies," he explained. "They be disorderly and quarrelsome, especially if they have obtained guns from the French in the north. 'Tis weak Josias, son of our old friend, Sachem Chickatawbut, who hath betrayed us. So we must look upon the Massachusetts also as our enemies."

"NO!" The sharp word came from young Know-God, who stood straight as an arrow beside Seaborn. "The Massachusetts be ever the English men's friends."

"He sayeth this because he is of their blood," cried the people.

"The Indian boy is right!" Widow Cummings now spoke. "The Massachusetts be the best friends the Colony hath!"

"How know ye?" "What said Owl Woman?" "Why tell ye not what news she brought?" "How know ye then, a newcomer, more about Indians than we who have lived among them for ten long years?" Discontented cries filled the air.

"What said the squaw, Mistress?" demanded Captain Stoddard.

"Tell it out at once!" ordered the Magistrate.

"Good sirs," said Widow Cummings calmly, "if I tell what ye wish to know, now, it will not help the Colony, but provoke undue alarm. Will ye then have me speak?"

The men frowned and turned away.

Captain Stoddard shouted to the Guard, ordering them to the fort. He sent all the other men to arm themselves and make preparations to defend the village against attack. He ordered the boys to bring all cows in from the common pasture and to fasten all domestic animals up in barns, sheds or lean-tos.

The Magistrate, Constable and tithing-men herded the women and children out of the meeting house. Like timid rabbits they scurried to the fort and huddled together with quaking hearts.

The palisade door was shut and barricaded with heavy

timbers. Captain Stoddard gave orders. With the supplies which had been brought, the women set to and boiled huge pots of samp and succotash. The boys began running bullets and mixing powder. The men took their weapons and mounted to the roof, ready to fire through loopholes.

But nothing happened. No Indians appeared.

On the third day in the week, tired out with the long waiting and having exhausted the food supply, the people were allowed to return to their homes under cover of darkness. Behind closed shutters and barred doors they continued to wait.

No one stirred in the village and no one stirred from the Partridge home. On the fourth day, Goodwife Partridge laid out breakfast and the family ate half-heartedly. Patty Tucker, in silence, washed up. Waitstill walked about, restless, and God-be-thanked cried fretfully, despite his mother's efforts to quiet him.

"How can we see the Indians when they come," asked Waitstill, "with all the shutters closed?"

"Who wants to see Indians?" cried Comfort.

"God will protect us," said Thankful softly.

Waitstill chose a moment when no one was looking. He climbed on a chair, opened a casement, unhooked the shutter and peeped out.

"I see *one* Indian!" he cried with delight.

"Waitstill!" cried Goodwife Partridge, panic-stricken.

"The Indians have come!" sobbed Comfort.

"God will protect us!" cried Thankful.

"He seeth Indians but in his imagination," laughed Patty. She went to the window and looked out over the boy's head. "He telled the truth," she added in a low voice. "An Indian cometh. He hath a gun, but he looks harmless enough."

The others hurried over and looked out.

"He looketh not like an enemy, with his English man's red coat!" laughed Aunt Charity.

"Why, 'tis our cow!" cried Comfort.

"Black Cloud leadeth our cow," added Thankful. "The danger is past. God hath delivered us."

"Black Cloud, our friend!" cried Waitstill happily. "I will open the shed door."

They all crowded round Black Cloud in the yard. He looked the same as usual, except that instead of bow and arrows, he carried a gun.

"Black Cloud find cow in meadow, eating tall hay grass," the Indian announced. "Black Cloud English man's friend. Bring cow back."

"The Massachusetts must then still be friendly," said Goodwife Partridge in a low voice. "But he hath a gun!"

"No matter!" said Aunt Charity. "They be friendly still. Of that I am confident."

"We will never forget Black Cloud's kindness," said Goodwife Partridge. "Come in and eat."

The man squatted on the hearth and ate greedily the food she set before him. "Ugh! Good!" he grunted. He looked round the darkened room. "Why sun hide his face in house?" he asked.

"The Indians . . ." began Waitstill.

"Hush, lad!" scolded his mother.

"Where Owl Woman?" asked Aunt Charity.

"Gone many arrow shots away," grunted Black Cloud. "When squaw come back?"

Black Cloud shook his head.

Soon he left the house, sauntering lazily down the winding path. He was a cause for wonder in the fear-stricken village. People peered out of their windows and watched him. His casual presence relieved the fears of many, but others seeing his gun, grew the more distrustful.

On the afternoon of the fifth day, Owl Woman returned.

The men had grown weary, but not lax with watching. No Tarratines had appeared and no Massachusetts. Josias, son of Chickatawbut, did not show his head. The little village, armed for combat, waited in vain for hostile Indians who never came.

Owl Woman went first to the Partridge home and told her news. She took a load of furs off her back and left them there. Then, with Widow Cummings by her side, she made haste to the Magistrate's house on the green. Captain Stoddard and all the leading men came to hear her story.

Widow Cummings spoke for her. "Ten days ago Know-God Humphrey appeared unexpectedly in the Indian village," she said. "He came to Sachem Cutshamekin to warn of coming trouble. He said a great army of Tarratines was on the march to wipe out the English men's colony by the sea. He said the Tarratine Sachem had been promised help of the Massachusetts by Josias, son of Chickatawbut.

"Cutshamekin, ever the friend of the English men, liked not this news. He was angered at his nephew's treachery. He called Owl Woman. He bade her leave her basket-making, go and make a friendly visit with the Tarratine squaws. He bade her keep her eyes open and find out from the squaws whether the Tarratines meant harm against the English men and their families. He sent Wuchowsen, a young brave, to offer black wolf-hides as a peace-offering to the Sachem of the Tarratines.

"Before she left, Owl Woman sought out Josias, the betrayer of his people. Josias, she knew, had taken rich gifts from the Tarratines, in return for which he made efforts to stir up the Massachusetts against the whites. But he had not succeeded. She told him so. She told him the Massachusetts were ever the friends of the white men.

She told him the white man's God would punish him for his betrayal of his people.

"Then she came to us. 'Twas during meeting on the Sabbath, as ye know," Widow Cummings went on. "She came to warn us of our danger."

The Magistrate interrupted: "Why then told ye us not what the Indian squaw said?"

"Owl Woman insisted the Tarratines were not yet on the war-path," answered Widow Cummings quietly. "I had no wish to alarm the people needlessly, for, like her, I had every reason to believe the mission of peace would succeed. My chief concern was to keep the people aware of the loyalty of the Massachusetts."

"Let us hear the rest of the squaw's story," said Captain Stoddard.

"She learned from the Tarratine squaws that an attack had indeed been planned. But when the Tarratine Sachem learned that he could not count on the help of the Massachusetts because of their never-wavering friendship for the English men, he accepted the wolf-hides from Wuchowsen and promised peace. He and his warriors have retired into their own territory. All danger is now over."

"But what of Josias, son of Chickatawbut?" asked the Magistrate. "Is he not still a dangerous enemy?"

With a broad smile, Owl Woman made answer: "Josias be afeared of white man's God. I tell him white man's God send small-pox on him, he die of small-pox like his father, Chickatawbut. Josias hath gone to live with the Mohawks in the west. He not want to see white men no more."

The men looked at each other with relief. They laughed and slapped each other on the back. They sent to Landlord Cluffe for sack and wine and drank thereof.

Black Cloud appeared at the Magistrate's door. He was called in, and he and his squaw were given a hearty meal to eat. Then they were presented with gifts—knives, beads, rolls of bright red cloth, and strings of purple and white wampum.

On their way back to the woods they stopped at the Partridge house, where Owl Woman unpacked the bundle of furs she had brought and presented Gaffer Partridge with forty beaver skins.

"For wolf-hide," she said, smiling. "Wolf-hide gone to Tarratine Sachem for peace-offering."

"Our wolf!" cried Waitstill.

"See, lass!" said Gaffer Partridge to Comfort. "The wolf ye feared so much hath helped to save the settlement."

"God's ways, indeed, be strange!" added Goodwife Partridge.

At supper that night, when Patty Tucker passed the trencherful of fried fish to Seaborn, he took several pieces in his fingers.

"I be nigh famished!" he cried. Then he looked up at Patty. "Ye told the truth about the Indians, Patty," he said. "I be right sorry I called thee a liar."

Patty curtsied and made no answer.

CHAPTER FIFTEEN

A Goodly
Heritage

Comfort Partridge had never been in the Magistrate's house before. Frightened and awed she walked by Aunt Charity's side and took her seat on the low form. Patty Tucker sat on Aunt Charity's left. Goodwife Partridge came in with the younger children and took the seat behind them.

Before the fireplace in the low-ceiled hall, Comfort saw a sturdy oak table covered with a red carpet. Web Avery, town clerk, sat at one end and Constable Cartwright, resplendent in all his armor, stood at the other, staff in hand.

It was the second Tuesday in October, town Court day. The hall was crowded with people. Women in gowns of russet, green and scarlet, wearing beaver hats or silken hoods or holland coifs, sat on forms or chairs. Men in broad white collars, red or green jerkins, cloth or leather breeches, beaver hats or Monmouth caps, and with bright red stockings on their legs, sat in chairs or leaned against the walls. Late-comers peered in at the open casement windows. Comfort felt sure that every one in Fair Haven By-the-Sea was there.

The buzz of conversation died down, as Magistrate Norris and Parson Humphrey entered and sat down in the two chairs behind the table. The charge against Seaborn Partridge came first. Comfort's heart began to pound.

"He hath neglected his duty as cow-keeper," read the clerk in a high-pitched voice, "left the town's cows by the roadside, so they entered a cornfield, did eat of the green corn whereof four of them died, for whose death he is held accountable. He hath reported an untrue rumor of an Indian attack."

Seaborn, seated on the opposite side of the room beside his father, stood up white-faced and anxious. Many people rose to his defence. It was quickly proved that he had not wilfully left the cows, but desired only to warn the settlement of approaching danger. And it was now well known by all that the danger had been a very real one.

Comfort settled back and breathed more easily.

Magistrate Norris disposed of the case. "Our young cow-keeper's second warning gave us time to arm against the Tarratine attack, which fortunately never came. Seaborn Partridge is discharged with honor."

The boy sat down in his place. Comfort turned and smiled at her mother.

The next case was read out: "Patience Tucker, redemptioner and servant maid, is charged with wilfully setting fire to her mistress' house and burning it to the ground."

Many witnesses raised their hands and swore to tell the truth, then rose to speak against her. Her character was first established. Poor Patty, thought Comfort. What a wicked, sinful girl she had been. Everything would go against her.

"I did see her oft running about the streets *in her hair,*" said Goodwife Rogers. "No respectable female appears at home or abroad without cap or coif."

"I catched her gadding at night after curfew," said the night Watchman. "She bit and scratched and kicked me in the performance of my duty."

"She reviled her mistress in my presence," cried Gershom Flagg, merchant. "She boasted of fine apparel above her station."

"She hath spoken evil of her mistress," testified Goodwife Minching, "from the first day she stepped off the boat."

People all over the audience jumped up.

"She said she hated her mistress," cried one.

"She wished never to lay eyes on her again," cried another.

"She wished her dead of small-pox!"

"She threatened oft to put a toad in her kettle of milk!"

The people laughed and Constable Cartwright pounded the floor with his staff for order.

"She told the children lies," testified the Constable's wife. "She told them fairy tales, idle songs, nursery rhymes and play-acting games such as still be common in Old England, but which all good Puritans frown upon."

"She hath sung ungodly songs and ballads," added Tithing-man Thatcher's wife. "She took them a-shroving . . ."

> *"A-shrovin', a-shrovin',*
> *I be come a-shrovin';*
> *A piece o' bread . . ."*

Waitstill's clear voice rang out unexpectedly, only to be smothered, as his mother hastily clapped her apron over his mouth.

"Silence!" boomed the Magistrate. "We must get to the main charges—the house-burning."

Goody Lumpkin nudged her husband with her elbow. "Get ye up and say what I told ye, lazy lout."

"Patty fed the pigs on the wort," piped Gaffer Lumpkin obediently, "so I didn't have no beer to drink."

"Not that, silly," whispered Goody Lumpkin. "Say she burnt the house down."

"She must a-set fire to it . . . there warn't no one else around," said Gaffer Lumpkin, shaking his head. "I don't see how she done it, unless she built up a roaring fire . . ."

"There warn't no fire in either fireplace when I went in," said Goodman Pettijohn. "The ashes was stone cold."

Seaborn Partridge raised his hand and spoke in a low voice: "Early that morn when I did see Patty Tucker, she was smoking a pipe of tobacco."

"A pipe! Tobacco!" cried the people, astonished.

Patty was called upon to explain: "The cornfield being unfenced, I obeyed my mistress' orders and went out to watch. I climbed up on the high oven behind the house, in order to see the better. I did but knock the ashes from my pipe, whereat the thatch did catch fire. I did not see the flames until I returned from the field, whither I went to drive out the cows."

She spoke in a quiet, calm voice. Comfort listened in surprise. She saw that the people were listening too.

"I did very wrong," continued Patty. "I did wrong to take pipe and tobacco from the Indians, but I never smoked much—it made me sick to stomach. I did wrong to knock the ashes out by the thatch, and thus through my carelessness, set fire to the house. My threats against my mistress were but idle, careless words. I did wrong never to try to pleasure her by willing obedience. I regret my sins and am resolved to mend my ways."

The people gasped. A penitent Patty Tucker they had never seen before. Perhaps she had only been careless, after all. Comfort felt very sorry for Patty, but the Magistrate did not.

"To wilfully set a house afire is a crime punishable by death," he said harshly. "The maid admits she did it not wilfully but carelessly. This act is but one of many careless deeds perpetrated by her since she was set ashore as a redemptioner. Her vice seems to be carelessness. Patience

Tucker is therefore sentenced to be set in the stocks for one hour upon the next Lecture Day, where she may be plainly seen by every lass and lad in the settlement, as a warning against carelessness. Also, she is to be returned to England on the next boat thereafter. Such ungodly servants we want not here among righteous folk."

Comfort's heart sank and tears came to her eyes. She saw Patty, with stricken face, sit down, overcome with despair. She looked at Aunt Charity, but her aunt made no move.

"One Jinny, wife of Gaffer Lumpkin," announced the clerk, "who by the violence of her tongue hath made his house and the neighborhood uncomfortable, is charged with being a notorious scold."

The people sat up briskly. At last Goody Lumpkin would get what she deserved. They'll put a cleft-stick on her tongue, thought Comfort.

From all over the room came plentiful testimony.

"She made a loud outcry in the public square on the day her pigs were intoxicated," cried Master Dillingham.

"She tittle-tattles," testified Tithing-man Thatcher. "She carries tales from house to house. Her tongue is loose at both ends."

"She made a loud outcry in my shop!" shouted Gershom Flagg.

"On the day her house burned down," boomed the Constable, "I heard her scold her serving maid, her husband and all her neighbors. I heard her revile Magistrate, Constable and Tithing-man."

"She hath abused her serving maid continually." Comfort was surprised to hear her mother speak. The people listened with respect to Goodwife Partridge's words. "She hath used Patience Tucker with brutality and unkindness. 'Tis a wonder the poor maid hath not perished under her cruel hands."

"True!" " 'Tis God's very truth!" murmured the women. "We have seen it often enough."

"She hath scolded her and hit her with the broomstaff daily," said one.

"She hath beat her with rods and oft with a whip," cried another.

"She fed her rotten victuals or starved her."

"She pommeled her, nipped, pinched and bruised her till she was black and blue. She shook the breath out of her."

"Ye lie!" shouted Goody Lumpkin, shaking her fist. "The Magistrate did order me to beat her oft. 'Tis the only way to git obedience."

"Silence!" ordered the Magistrate. "Thy very words condemn thee, woman! Are there any to speak in Goodwife Lumpkin's defence?"

No one rose. Silence filled the room.

"For being a notorious scold," said the Magistrate, "I do sentence ye, Jinny Lumpkin, to be set in the ducking-stool and dipped over head and ears in some convenient place of fresh or salt water as oft as necessary to cool the immoderate heat of thy tongue."

Goody Lumpkin began to moan aloud, but at a sharp glance from the Magistrate ceased abruptly.

"The testimony just given throws new light upon the case of Patience Tucker, redemptioner," continued the

Magistrate. "Patience Tucker, have ye any charge to make against thy mistress? Have ye been used with cruelty, beaten beyond endurance?"

Patty rose. All the hatred she had felt for her mistress welled up within her, and all her dread of returning to England. But ugly thoughts of revenge faded away as she remembered Mistress Charity's counsels. She thought of Shrovetide and how the happy children had made her know that Goody Lumpkin could never hurt her again.

"Nay, good sir," replied Patty. "I bring no charge against her."

She sat down. Once more the people murmured. Magistrate Norris whispered to Parson Humphrey. Comfort twisted her handkercher in her hands. Once she had thought Patty wicked and sinful. Now she knew how brave and unselfish she was. If only Patty could stay . . .

The audience stirred visibly when Widow Cummings was called and came forward. She wore her London mulberry gown with the full sleeves and lace ruffles. She wore embroidered gloves on her hands and the beaver hat with the pearl band on her head.

"Mistress Charity Cummings, gentlewoman," read the clerk, "is charged with corrupting the youth by teaching them to keep Christmas, go a-shroving, a-maying and other vicious practices which tend to the nourishment of vice."

Comfort thought her aunt had never looked so beautiful. She gazed at her with loving pride, and her heart beat fast with a desire to protect her from all those who would do her harm.

The testimonies began.

"She hath turned up her nose at the stench of soft soap boiling," said Goodwife Minching. "I did reprove her, but she gave me flippant answers."

"Look ye! Her coif is embroidered with cut-work," cried Mistress Cartwright, pointing. "Her bodice is stiffened with whalebone stays, her neck-cloth hath lace on the edge."

"She told the childer of Christmas in Old England," said Goodwife Seward. "She helped them to fetch greenery, bake Yule cakes, play games, sing mirthful songs that were not psalms."

"She hid wheaten flour in her sea-chest," cried Goodwife Thatcher. "She made Shrovetide pancakes and fed them to the childer."

"She took them a-maying," added Goodwife Eliot. "She teached them May-games."

"She set up a Maypole," announced Parson Humphrey, "and they danced round it and sang."

An awkward silence fell. No one could think of more to say. Comfort's heart pounded. How could they say such joyous occasions were wrong, when the children loved them so much? If only children were allowed to testify . . . Then she found herself on her feet, with a sea of faces staring at her.

"Good sir," the words came of themselves, "the childer were never so happy in all their lives before—they loved Christmas and Shrovetide and May Day—they loved Aunt Charity's songs and games, and Patty Tucker's too! They were never so happy in all their days before . . ."

"Silence!" boomed the Magistrate. "Children speak not except when spoken to!"

Comfort sat down in confusion. She was trembling from head to foot. It was an unheard-of thing to do, but she had to speak because of her great love for Aunt Charity. If punishment came, she would not care. Now that it was over, Comfort was glad. Then she listened.

"Ye want your children to have no happiness then?" Aunt Charity was saying. "By my faith, ye Puritans sicken my stomach! Ye would make lisping saints and mournful hypocrites out of babes in their very cradles. Ye would deny them all the joys of childhood. Running, laughing, babbling, cackling, playing, jumping—all these be wrong and evil!

"What sour, sad-faced men and women ye have become! What a change this land hath wrought! Ye never had such thoughts before. Ye yourselves ran and romped and played and laughed and sang. Ye babbled and frisked about when ye were young. May not thy children do the same?

"Christmas, Shrovetide, May Day—ye loved them well, yet now ye do deny them. I confess my guilt in teaching these practices to thy children, for I see no wrong in them. Therefore am I the more glad that I have planted the seeds of these joyous festivals in thy children's hearts. That they may sprout to bear fruit in thy children's children's children, is my prayerful hope."

The people were amazed to hear such bold words, and could not but admire the woman's courage. Comfort felt assured.

"These offenses be grave indeed," said the Magistrate. "Ye encourage evil practices which the Colony hath abolished. Such a course, Mistress, cannot continue. Ye strike deeply at the welfare of the Colony when ye harm its children."

"Sir, I do not believe that to be so," answered Widow Cummings quietly. "None hath greater love for your children than I. Love enricheth their lives. They respond to love with light-heartedness, even as a bird responds to sunshine with song. Let them be gay and happy while they may, for soon, too soon, will the mantle of stern maturity fall upon them. Truly there is no pleasure comparable to a generous spirit.

"We came to this fair land to build a new world, a *New* England. If I then look back to the Old, if I remind you of the life we lived there, 'tis because I wish to preserve the best in the old ways for a goodly heritage. Do away with Old England's wrongs, I beg you, but hold fast to its good, and make your new world the richer."

She turned to the people. "Have I then harmed a single one of your children? If so, speak out."

The women looked at each other, as memories came crowding.

"She hath saved my daughter Temperance from the jaws of Death," cried Mistress Seward.

"She hath learned my Silence to talk and smile," said Goodwife Pitkin.

"She hath changed my timid, shrinking son into a brave and forward boy," cried Goodwife Rogers.

"She hath teached me how to return good for evil," spoke up Patty Tucker.

"She sat up night after night with us, when the winter's sickness came," said Mistress Hollingworth. "This we shall always remember."

"She went to the Indian village in a blizzard and brought the squaw with her medicine bag to cure our children," said Goodwife Thatcher. "How can we ever forget?"

" 'Twas her friendship for Owl Woman which kept the Massachusetts Indians loyal," spoke up Constable Cartwright.

Comfort leaned close to Patty Tucker and grasped her hand. Aunt Charity had friends, after all.

The Magistrate conferred with Parson Humphrey and others of the men in low tones during a short intermission. Then the Magistrate spoke:

"There seems to be no doubt but that Widow Cummings hath more than done her duty among us. She hath, since her arrival on the *Fearless* just one year ago, served the settlement with devotion and loyalty. She hath shown mercy with cheerfulness and ministered to the sick and poor brethren—as a childless widow should. More than that, she hath in twelve short months become the beloved of all our children. Her influence upon them hath on the whole been good. But . . ." He frowned, then continued:

"These festivals—Christmas, Shrovetide, May Day and the like, these the Colony hath forbidden and wants not revived. As we all know, their celebration in Old England has long been a time of debauchery and drunkenness. That is the reason we forbid them here."

"These days, good sir, have indeed been abused by *adults* in Old England," replied Widow Cummings. "But can they not be changed into happy, harmless, playful celebrations for *children* in this new country? Our life here is so cold and austere, there is little to pleasure the children. Cannot New England take the best of these old festivals and preserve it for the children of the future?"

"The Colony hath forbidden them by law," retorted the Magistrate in a stern voice. "The Colony hath instituted Thanksgiving Day and Election Day to supersede them."

"I see no wrong in them," said Widow Cummings, "but if ye forbid them, I abide by your law. But—to forbid me to love the children, that ye cannot. Forbid me to encourage their light-heartedness, that ye cannot. These children will build in this fair land a great nation . . . Ye shall not crush out their spirits . . ."

The Magistrate interrupted abruptly: "The Governor of the Colony hath ordered that schools be set up in ye towns for the better training of our youth. A Dame School for the younger children is greatly desired in our fair town." He turned to the people. "Will ye send your childer to Widow Cummings, schooldame?"

"Ay, good sir!" "Ay, that we will!" came the cries.

"Will ye consent, Mistress, when a suitable building is provided, to conduct a Dame School in our midst?"

"Good sir, it would pleasure me right well," answered Widow Cummings, "for the welfare of little children lies close to my heart. I can undertake it, however, under only one condition. By reason that the children be many and the work arduous, I will need a capable assistant. May I then have the help of young Patty Tucker?"

Patty jumped up, her dejection gone and a broad smile of hope on her face. "Oh, Mistress!" she cried. Happy tears ran down her cheeks. "I'll serve ye till my dying day!"

"Patty Tucker!" "Redemptioner!" "Sentenced to be stocked and sent back to England!" The people gasped.

How easy to remember the evil about Patty and to forget the good, thought Comfort.

"The case of Patience Tucker, redemptioner, will now be resumed," said the Magistrate. "It hath been established that the maid's wickedness was largely provoked by the brutality of her mistress. The severity of her sentence may therefore be somewhat alleviated. Are ye willing that the maid be given a chance to mend her ways?"

"I'll sit in ye stocks, good sir," cried Patty, jumping to her feet again, "if only ye won't send me back to Old

England. 'Tis *New* England I love!"

"I have found Patty ever willing, obedient and cheerful," said Widow Cummings, "when she is treated with kindness. She hath an engaging and steadfast love of children. They run to her instinctively because she loves and understands them." She looked about on the crowd. "If there be any who doubt or mistrust her, let me say that I will stand responsible for her conduct and guarantee that your children will be in as good hands with her as with me. Do ye trust me?"

"Ay, Mistress!" "Ay, that we do!" came the assenting voices.

The Magistrate now turned to Patty.

"You are now free of your former master and mistress, Patience Tucker," he said. "To send you back to Old England would be to return you to a life of wickedness and evil. To keep you here, as assistant to Widow Cummings, our schooldame, will, we hope, make you an honest woman, a credit to the Colony and an honor to God."

"Thank ye, good sir!" replied Patty.

Then before all the crowd, she threw her arms round Mistress Charity's neck. Comfort looked on, smiling. She could not speak for happiness.

.   .   .   .

On the following Thursday, after Lecture, a crowd of people gathered on the river bank. Goody Lumpkin was taken there by Constable Cartwright, who was joined by Magistrate Norris and Parson Humphrey. She was placed upon the ducking-stool, fastened down with cords, and her feet were tied fast together. The Constable then slackened the ropes and allowed her to sink down under the water for the space of half a minute. Goody Lumpkin came up screaming and scolding. She was ducked again, and again. After the fifth time, she caught her breath and cried out: "Let me go, good sirs. By God's help, I will sin no more."

Whereupon the machine was withdrawn, the ropes were untied and the woman released.

On the same afternoon, Patty Tucker, redemptioner, sat alone in the stocks on the village green. When a woman in wet clothes passed by, Patty recognized her former mistress.

"I be right sorry, Goody!" she exclaimed.

The woman did not trust herself to speak. She patted the girl on the shoulder as a sign of forgiveness, then walked slowly away to her English wigwam beside the sea.

A few weeks later, the Dame School opened in a small building on the village green. Patty Tucker, resplendent in red gown, holland coif and apron, and flowered neckcloth, greeted the children.

"*Our* Patty!" cried Waitstill and all the others, as they trooped in at the door.

THE END

BIBLIOGRAPHY

OLD ENGLISH SOURCES

Earle, Alice Morse—*Margaret Winthrop*, 1895
Godfrey, Elizabeth—*English Children in the Olden Time*, 1907
—— *Home Life Under the Stuarts*
—— *Social Life Under the Stuarts*
Harrison, Wm.—*Elizabethan England (1577-87)*, 1876
Hartley, Dorothy, and Elliot, Margaret M.—*Life and Works of the People of England, 16th Century*, 1926
Quennell, M. and C. H. B.—*A History of Everyday Things in England* (1500-1799), 3 vols. 1918-1935
Sainliens (Claudius Hollyband), and Erondell, Peter—*The Elizabethan Home*
Stephenson, Henry Thew—*The Elizabethan People*, 1910
Strutt, Joseph—*The Sports and Pastimes of the People of England*, 1801 (1903 edition)
Traill, H. D., and Mann, J. S.—*Social England*, vols. III & IV, 1895
Tusser, Thomas—*Good Husbandry*
Verney Family—*Memoirs*

ORIGINAL SOURCES

Bradford, William—*History of Plymouth Plantation, 1607-1648*, published 1856
Clap, Roger—*Memoirs, 1630*, published 1731
Lechford, Thos.—*Plain Dealing or News from New England 1642*, published 1867

222

Morton, Thos.—*New English Canaan,* 1636

Smith, Capt. John—*Works,* containing:
A Description of New England
Advertisements for the Unexperienced or The Path-way
to Erect a Plantation, 1631

Winthrop, John—*Journals,* 2 vols. 1630-49, published 1908

Wood, Wm.—*New England's Prospect,* 1634

Young, Alexander—*Chronicles of the Pilgrim Fathers from*
1602-25, published 1841

The Founding of Massachusetts: *A Selection from the*
Sources of the History of the Settlement 1628-31, pub-
lished 1930; Containing:
Higginson—*True Relation*
———— *New England's Plantation*

SECONDARY NEW ENGLAND SOURCES

Briggs, Martin S.—*The Homes of the Pilgrim Fathers in*
England and America (1620-1685), 1932

Byington, Ezra Hoyt—*The Puritan in England and New*
England, 1900

Dow, George Francis—*Every Day Life in the Massachusetts*
Bay Colony, 1935

Earle, Alice Morse—*Child Life in Colonial Days,* 1899
———— *Curious Punishments of Bygone Days,* 1896
———— *Customs and Fashions in Old New England,* 1893
———— *Home Life in Colonial Days,* 1898
———— *Margaret Winthrop,* 1895
———— *The Sabbath in Puritan New England,* 1893

Fisher, S. G.—*Men, Women and Manners in Colonial*
Times, 1898

Fiske, John—*The Beginnings of New England,* 1895

Hart, Albert Bushnell, Ed.—*American History Told by Contemporaries,* 1900

Howe, Daniel Wait—*The Puritan Republic,* 1899

Langdon, Wm. Chauncy—*Everyday Things in American Life (1607-1776),* 1937

Morison, Samuel Eliot—*The Puritan Pronaos,* 1936

Weeden, Wm. B.—*Economic and Social History of New England (1620-1789),* 1891